Summary

This is a story of two childhood friends named Wicked and Evil who are from Cleveland, Ohio. Their friendship will be tested through multiple circumstances as Wicked is forced to do prison time. Wicked will go through the birth of a new baby girl, betrayal, trust, and love to come out to be the man he was determined to be.

LOYALTY IS ROYALTY

*"Nothing Beats the Cross but
The Double Cross."*

Two best friends named Wicked and Evil had their lives turned upside down by unexpected events. When Wicked faces a prison sentence and the imminent arrival of his daughter, he must confront the harsh reality of his future. Little did he know, he was in for a rude awakening when he discovers that his childhood friend's betrayal would hit him like a ton of bricks. Will their friendship survive the ultimate test of loyalty, or will it crumble under the weight of betrayal?

Acknowledgment

I want to give special thanks to my family and friends for holding me down and believing in me. I love y'all my wonderful children, Mercedes, Maurice Jr., Marquise, and the rest of the family. My brother from another Mother Keith Adams Sr. without you there's no me! Tri-Clopse Inc. To my beloved mother, Robbie Jean Jackson (RIP), you are my guardian angel. And to my beautiful wife, Tanya Monique Hamilton-Jackson (RIP). A special thanks to Meagan Spark my heart and soul, you know I love you. My step kids Fatty, Weez, and Pooh, and thank you Baby girl (LaChrisha). Thanks to everybody that told me to keep writing and fighting. I heard y'all loud and clear. Thanks, Premeer LLC, and my entire world Ms. Alicia Skinner aka Poohna I love you, Cuz!!!! Be on the lookout for more from Premeer LLC.

Table of Contents

Prologue

This story is about two childhood friends named Wicked and Evil who are from Cleveland, Ohio. Their friendship will be tested through multiple circumstances as Wicked is forced to do prison time. Wicked will go through the birth of a new baby girl, betrayal, trust, and love to come out to be the man he was determined to be. What keeps Wicked strong is the power of family and his pops, Big Moose who helps him stay on track with his life and goals. Wicked sees and knows who is there for him and who is not. He loses friends and gains some along the way, but family and success were his main priority. Now he must figure out how to move forward in the rage of having revenge against Evil....

Chapter 1:

Happy Birthday

It was a cold November morning as young Wicked got dressed to visit his father in prison. This was the first time that Wicked was going to visit his father by himself. Today was Wicked's 18th birthday, and he has a baby girl on the way. He couldn't wait to share the news with his dad. As the time seemed to move at a rapid pace, Wicked reached for the blunt from last night. He could still smell the aroma from the exotic that filled the blunt. Now the only thing that was missing from last night was Meagan's fine ass. Meagan is Wicked's baby momma, and she is a street thug's dream. She is 5' 6," caramel complexion with them Asian slanted cat eyes that were light greyish/hazel brown. She has high cheekbones with big full lips that looked like she has been getting collagen injections her whole life. Her true assets were her scandalous body which made her measurements (36D, 26, and 44) if you know what I mean. Let's just say the girl is bad, and Wicked wouldn't have it any other way.

Once Wicked hit his blunt of that gas, he quickly remembered that he has not seen his father in over a year. Although he will be upset because he hasn't seen his son in over a year, he will still be happy he's there to see him. Wicked's pops is serving a 30-year sentence for some gun and drug charges. Wicked emerged from the shower and donned his latest Gucci outfit that Meagan had gifted him for his birthday. Wicked stood in front of this full-length mirror and told himself that he was going to start working out because he knew his pops was going to be talking shit about him only weighing 178 pounds. Although in Wicked's mind, nobody would step to him sideways in the streets. See, one thing about Wicked; he was no fool, and he had a reputation that was second to none. He has a gang of pretty lil bitches that loved his dirty draws. Wicked wasn't worried about his pops or anybody in the streets. He got dressed and told Meagan he would be back in a few hours after seeing his pops.

Young Wicked, all grown up now jumped in his black-on-black 2012' Range Rover with matte black rims with the factory tint. Wicked went to Mansfield Correctional Institution a little after 10 am. Shortly thereafter, Wicked's pops came strolling out to the visiting room area. Once Wicked's pops saw his now grown son, both men stood and hugged each other like a father and son would. Wicked's pops looked at his son up and down and said, "damn son, I see you done grown up on me overnight." Wicked was feeling good from his pop's approval acknowledging him as a grown-up man. Now, Wicked's pops whom the streets call "Big Homie" or "Big Moose" told his son that he is proud of him and wished that he would come to see him more often. Wicked is proud of his pops and even though he was gone for so long, the streets still had so much love for him. Let's be honest; the main reason why Wicked was able to secure that Mexican connection that he got was because of who his pops was. Those eses loved Big Moose, and the amount of weight he was moving.

Not to mention the fact that Big Moose went to trial and never mentioned anybody's name at trial even after the government charged him with the (R.I.C.O.) Act. He was facing life in prison. Nevertheless, Wicked always admired his pops street credibility, and the fact that his pops has been holding it down from the joint for 12 straight years. Now it was Wicked who had to tell his pops not only that it was his 18th

Birthday, but his girl was pregnant. Big Moose is about to be a grandfather, as he listened to his son express his excitement about becoming a father himself. Big Moose's eyes got glossy from his own joy hearing how his son has grown up. Big Moose sat and marveled at his young son's ability to identify with life, and all the things that life has to offer. He reminded himself how the apple didn't fall far from the tree.

Big Moose told Wicked that he has been hearing Wicked's name ringing in the streets about a lot of drugs and gun activity. Wicked has always suspected that his father had heard about his few run-ins with the police or bitch ass Kats in the streets. Now, Wicked wondered if his mother had told Big Moose about his movements. Wicked's mother is a gangster in her own right. Young Wicked loved his mother like Tony Montana loved his sister in the movie "Scarface." She has been riding with Big Moose his whole bid and Wicked admired her for her loyalty to his pops. Big Moose has his own lil' female who would come to Mansfield and make sure he was straight on whatever he needed. He has the latest iPhone that was out, so he was up on games with Facebook & Instagram. The COs made an announcement; "all visitors have five minutes left, so start saying your goodbyes." Both Big Moose and Wicked became overwhelmed with sadness neither one wanting the other to detect their emotional state stood up and hugged each other tightly. As the visit drew to a close, Big Moose wished Wicked a happy birthday and expressed his love for his son, reminding him to stay safe out there. As Wicked listened to his pops, he quickly cut him off and said pops I'm good and I love you too. You keep holding it down in here, and we're still working on getting you out. . The crowd and visitors left the prison.

 Big Moose told himself that he was extremely proud of his son as he went back to get stripped and searched. As Wicked drove away from the prison, all he could think about was how strong his pops was. He was doing all that time and still standing strong. Just as he reached for his sack of gas, his phone started vibrating out of control. As he looked at the phone, he saw that he had 26 missed calls. Most of the calls were from the usual suspects (Robin, Boo, Ashley, Selina, and Brittany). See, these are all Wicked's lil' females, and they all loved this man with real loyalty. Today is Wicked's birthday, and all he wanted to do was spend this weekend with his baby momma Meagan. It is about two weeks since Wicked has been in the city because he had gone to Miami to handle some shit that he had to complete with his right-hand man Evil. So, Wicked being a man of his word had promised Meagan his attention once he had gotten back to Cleveland, Ohio. It was 4:05 pm, and the weather was acting crazy today. The temperature has dropped down to about 18 degrees which is very cold for November. Everyone from Ohio was used to this unpredictable weather.

Wicked drove home in deep thought as he contemplated his plans for his birthday party tonight. The silence was broken when he hit the remote, and Lil Boosie came blasting out the speakers. As Meagan reached to grab her phone to call her man to see where he was, she stopped and thought to herself, then decided that she would run to the jewelry store to get that Cuban link that Wicked had seen and fallen in love with when they were in Atlanta a few months ago. See, Meagan was thorough in every regard, and she loved her man. She knew that Wicked loved her the same. This bond that they shared made her public enemy number one in the eyes of all Wicked's side bitches, and a few bitch ass wannabe. By Meagan being so game-tight, she was aware of all her haters. This gave her the ability to strive harder from her hater's energy. So, she decided to jump in her all-silver 2013 G-Wagon. Meagan was self-made. She is a young entrepreneur that had the game from her mother who inherited a large sum of money from an insurance payout and has never looked back. Meagan's mother remarried after Meagan's father died in a motorcycle accident.

Young Meagan is light years ahead of most females her age. Plus, she has a vision in life, and she always sees Wicked in her future. As she pulled up in the mall's parking lot, she smiled to herself knowing that Wicked was going to put the pound game down on her once he saw this chain she was getting him on his birthday. Meagan parked the G-Wagon and went inside the jewelry store where the woman greeted her with a bottle of champagne. She had spoken to her previously on the phone. Both women made their way to the back of the store to look at the jewelry on display. Meagan has an extraordinary eye for the best fashion out.

Chapter 2:

Shots Fired

Wicked fired up the blunt he had just got his hands on and inhaled that smooth smoke and damn near coughed out his seafood from yesterday. Wicked said to himself damn, I miss this throwback exotic. He was doing about 90 in his silver Maserati and almost got stopped by the boys for speeding, but Wicked saw the cruiser just in time to slow his ass down. Wicked made it to Evil's house in no time rolling in that Maserati. Evil was already waiting on Wicked, so as soon as Wicked pulled into the driveway, Evil jumped straight in the whip and Wicked sped off. Their phones started ringing and vibrating at the same damn time, and each one was setting plays in motion, directing traffic like two Mexican Cartel members. Wicked and Evil complimented each other well because they were night and day when it comes to personalities. When it comes to crunching numbers, they were also second to none. Evil had just finished talking to his guy in Cincinnati and was telling Wicked that his guy wanted 25 bricks ASAP. That he has his little cousin's crew in Akron that was ready for 20.

As Wicked listened to his homeboy run off these figures, it was Wicked who had been waiting to tell Evil how his redbone Selina had just moved 30 bricks the first night they had landed in Cleveland, and that's why she wasn't at the party. Evil smiled at his partner and admired how Wicked always seemed to be ten steps ahead of the game. See, what Evil did not realize was that Wicked got his game from his pops and his mom. Evil on the other hand got his game from Wicked! The maserati began to slow down and Wicked told Evil, "That they were at the spot." As they exited the car, Wicked knew that this move was going to solidify his status as the King in the streets. Leaning out of the window from the second floor, a young Mexican boy said, "hey over here homes." Wicked and Evil walked towards the building that looked vacant. The door opened and both men went inside. Once inside, Hector was sitting on the couch talking in Spanish on the phone. Hector motioned both Wicked and Evil to sit with him on the couch. Two female Mexican women came from the back room and quickly left through the front door. For some strange reason, Mexicans did not like doing business in front of their women ever. One day Wicked asked Hector why women weren't allowed to sit in on their transactions. Hector told Wicked that in his country, women are viewed as weak and would tell everything if they were ever tortured or wanted to betray their husbands for adultery. So, a woman is never allowed to know the business of any cartel member, or she must die.

After processing that info, Wicked always made sure no female knew the ins and outs of his business. Wicked had conveyed this info to Evil a while ago when Evil's girl had asked him about his business affairs. Wicked had told Evil to check his girl, but Evil had figured Wicked was overreacting. Hector's little brother Louis came into the room with two black duffle bags with 125 bricks in each bag. Louis, who Wicked has always gotten along with tossed the bags to Wicked and said, "here you go homies, the world is yours now." Both Hector and Louis told Wicked and Evil that those bricks were 86 percent pure so one could make two.

Wicked said to himself; these Mexican muthafuckers got it going on. Hector assured Wicked and Evil that this is the deal of a lifetime. We're doing it because of Big Moose who we love forever and we should look after his son. So, as Hector told Wicked and Evil that he wanted twenty thousand for each brick when this being 2012 and bricks going for twenty-five, it was a no brainer for Wicked and Evil to see their money instantly. Everybody agreed on the price and the arrangements. Hector and Louis both said we'll be in touch. Wicked drove across the street and called AAA towing to move his Maserati that has a life sentence in it. As the two men waited on the tow service to move the car, they decided that now would be a suitable time to use their burner phones and get the troops on deck. They called everybody in every city and lined up about 150 bricks to be gone by tomorrow. This is what made them two click because nobody could hustle as a team better than Wicked and Evil. Within an hour they were on their way riding up front in the tow truck as 250 kilos (about three days) of 86 percent pure cocaine was being hauled for them free of charge. Not to mention no risk on their behalf. Evil was smiling as the tow truck drove through the traffic. Wicked asked Evil what he was smiling at, and Evil said, "Man you never cease to amaze me with your sharp-ass mind. I would have never thought of getting a tow truck to deliver our drugs for us." Wicked told Evil "Can't no nigga hustle like you and remain loyal."

The day was going faster by the minute and both Wicked and Evil were busy lining sales up to sell those bricks that were fresh off the press. It always seemed to turn into a friendly competition between Wicked and Evil to see who could push the most product no matter what it was. Evil was making moves with his crew on the west side of Cleveland that was mostly Hispanics. They were always good business for Evil and he could rely on them to grab 30 at a time. But this time with Evil and Wicked flipping them 250 into 500 and shit was still A-1 how could they lose by selling the bricks at a price nobody could refuse. Wicked and Evil decided to have Wicked's uncle and his crew in Columbus whip 250 into 500 and pay them one hundred thousand for their help. So, now instead of having the original 250 bricks, Wicked and Evil now sat on 500 grade-A fish scale kilos . So, today Evil has the Ricans in the palm of his hands because everybody that was hustling in the streets knew that the average brick was going for 25 to 28 thousand all day. Evil realized that Ricans sold 100 bricks at 22 apiece. At this price everybody was happy. Meanwhile, on the other side of town, Wicked was dropping 40 bricks off to his stepbrother who was a few years younger than Wicked, but a solid hustler. Wicked knew that his time was limited because he would be attending a party in Cleveland later that night and he knew that he also wanted to be in Columbus for the concert the next day. Evil had texted and asked Wicked to meet him at the spot. An hour later Wicked was pulling into their honeycomb hideout in Shaker Heights, a suburb on the outskirts of Cleveland. Both Wicked and Evil had just dumped over 280 bricks in Cleveland alone. Plus, the 40 to 50 in Akron and another 50 in Lorain, Ohio. Now the two of them sat back and said to each other at the same time, damn we just downed over 300 bricks and most of what they had was already pre-paid.

Now the two of them feeling good about their business decided to go out for a few drinks and mingle with some bitches. Wicked called his stepbrother, they called Reese and told him that they were going to the "MIRAGE ON THE WATER," so be there or be square. Reese, knowing how Wicked liked to splurge, called a few more family members and told them to come to the MIRAGE because Wicked and Evil were going to be there. Wicked had gotten a call from Meagan and she told Wicked that she was going to the hospital because her contraction was coming more frequently and they were intense. Wicked told Evil that Meagan might be having the baby sooner than expected. Evil, who was already proud of a little girl himself told Wicked that they would shoot to Grove Port to make sure Meagan and the baby would be ok. However Wicked said let's hit this club up first and if Meagan calls back then he would be on his way to be by his baby momma's side. So, Wicked and Evil made one more stop and put the money they had just removed from a spot they used from time to time to a spot that the two of them only knew about. They carried five duffle bags of money into this safe house way out in the middle of uninhabited land that was surrounded by a bunch of farmlands. Wicked and Evil had just dropped off 1.2 million in cash and had plenty more where that came from. So, as they left the safe house, they both decided that the rest of the night was all about celebrating.

Wicked dropped Evil off at one of his bitches' houses where Evil kept a money green 71' Chevelle parked inside of her garage. Evil has a thing for Monique the chocolate short body that had him sprung from that good wet pussy he bragged about constantly. Wicked, knowing he was about to be a father, made his way to Selina's house. Selina has been waiting for her moment with Wicked since they were in Columbus three weeks ago right before Wicked went to Miami. Selina was Wicked's both pride and joy because with her he had the best of both worlds. Selina was living like one of the homies Wicked would kick it with. She is one of the best money-getters (male or female), but she is a pretty ass redbone bitch that fucked like a porn star and Wicked loved every minute he shared with Selina. Wicked pulled up at Selina's house ready for the battle ahead of him. He has his own key to her house, so he let himself in. Selina was taking a shower, so he walked into the bathroom. Selina didn't know Wicked was standing behind the shower glass. He scared her in a clever way by pulling the glass open. Wicked made Selina get out of the shower and he told her to strip him down and she did just that. Selina sucked Wicked's dick like it was a new flavor popsicle, and Wicked sucked her pussy like it was a piece of steak with A-1 sauce on it. They sucked and fucked for at least an hour.

It was 10:45 pm and Wicked and Selina left her house headed to The Mirage On The Water. This is one of Cleveland's best live night clubs the city has to offer and Wicked knew that he has to show up and show out. He decided to wear an Off-White Denim outfit. Wicked had on a Rolex watch and a Rolex chain with Louis Vuitton shades. He finished this look off with a pair of dark blue Gucci loafers. Wicked knew that he looked like a million dollars. But, more importantly, he felt like a G worth a million dollars! As Wicked and Selina pulled into the parking lot, they both noticed that there had to be at least 500 people just chilling in the parking lot getting their drinks and smoke on. Wicked has always enjoyed being late for an event and people would always say "nigga you gone be late for your own funeral." But what everyone did not realize was Wicked felt like he was the party, so it didn't start until he got there anyway.

Selina looked at the crowded parking lot and said to Wicked damn babe it feels so right being with you knowing all these hoes want you. Wicked knew Selina was telling the truth because so many bitches yearn to be with the young gangster. The Mirage On The Water is the place to be in Cleveland and as Wicked maneuvered his gold 66' Camaro, he knew all eyes were on him. The crowd in the parking lot seemed to have gotten larger by the time Wicked parked his old school. As they made their way towards the entrance, he saw Brittany who was Boo's sister, and she quickly ran up to Wicked demanding a hug. Wicked hadn't seen Brittany since the summer and now it was November. They all walked into the club together, but Wicked was arm and arm with Selina who wouldn't have it any other way. Once inside, Evil spotted Wicked and shouted across the bar, "there goes the realist nigga breathing if I hold my breath." Wicked smiled and nodded at his homie who he has mad love for. Evil waived to the bartender and ordered a case of Ace of Spades for him and his bro. Everybody was at this club tonight and Wicked saw all his stepbrothers and sister. Pooh, Wicked's sister was there with her man that didn't appeal to Wicked. Selina was playing her position and she was all over Wicked like a sweaty pair of draws on his ass. Selina wanted every bitch in the club to know that she was with Wicked tonight so back the fuck up! Brittany in her see-through dress stepped towards Wicked and all that ass sticking out on that little ass frame had Wicked stuck, as she said what's up bro? Wicked, remembering how she always swallowed all his nut every time she sucked his dick said I'm good doing me out her (feel me). Brittany shook her head in approval, still trying to get Wicked away from his security guard Selina. But to Brittany's surprise, Wicked grabbed her arm and pulled her onto the dance floor where everybody else followed. Now the club was really rocking. Wicked and Brittany made their chemistry seem like they were lifelong dance partners.

Wicked always enjoyed fucking with Brittany, she was cool as fuck to hang out with. Plus, she had gotten Wicked his first major plug with them Jamaicans five years ago when he first jumped off the porch selling pounds of mid. Evil was fucking it up on the dance floor too, and he had in his mind that he wasn't going to let Wicked outdo him tonight. He has his chocolate thing on the dance floor going ham! Evil was doing all the latest dances that were out. The club was a success and as the club was ending, Wicked told Evil that he needed to go to Columbus to be with

Meagan and make it to that concert. Everybody knew Wicked was a Lil Boosie fan and ever since Lil Boosie had dropped Touched Down to Cause Hell, the streets were going crazy and Wicked has to be a part of that being an up-and-coming rapper himself. He had opened for a few artists like Drake, TI, and Lil Wayne. But what Wicked was really thinking about was that baby girl of his that was coming any day now! Once Mirage On The Water closed, Wicked dropped Selina off and told her he would have instructions for her about the rest of that weight in a few days. Wicked called Evil and told him he was on his way to Columbus.

It was 4:20 in the morning and it didn't seem like anybody else in the world was awake as Wicked drove down 71 south heading to Columbus. He got home in less than two hours as he drove his old school home. After driving for a few hours, Wicked was extremely tired and just wanted to get some sleep. Meagan was sound asleep and Wicked not wanting to wake her up slid out of his clothes and climbed into the bed next to his girl. Later that day, Wicked was awakened by the smell of turkey bacon and blueberry pancakes along with some sunny-side-up eggs and Texas toast. Meagan was making Wicked's plate when he walked up behind her and held her around her waist. Meagan always loved when her man showed her that type of affection. Wicked had told Meagan on the phone last night that he loved her, but Meagan was thinking to herself while she lay in bed that Wicked was just drunk and was feeling himself from all the Hennessy he was drinking.

So, Meagan saw this as an excellent opportunity to ask Wicked if he really meant what he said on the phone last night. As she watched Wicked devour the food she had prepared, she said babe let me ask you something. Wicked said, "what's up babe?" Meagan looked at him dead center in the eyes and asked him "DO YOU LOVE ME?" She said before you answer this, I really need you to understand what I just asked you. Wicked, seeing that his girl was serious looked at her and said in a low smooth voice, "Babe I've been loving you and I Love You even more now since you're the mother of my baby girl." Meagan's heart sank down to her stomach and she jumped up and squeezed Wicked around the neck so tight he thought she was going to break his shit. It was at that very moment that Meagan knew in her heart of hearts that Wicked was truly the man she needed and would stand by her man no matter what. Little did Meagan know Wicked was saying the exact same thing about his girl.

As Wicked finished his food, Megan ran him some bath water and put his clothes out for the day. After Wicked got dressed in one of his Gucci fits, he asked Meagan if she remembered that he was going to the Lil Boosie concert tonight. Meagan had indeed forgotten about the concert, and she was saddened because she thought that they would spend the day together. Meagan couldn't remember the last time they were a family together. So, Meagan decided to have Wicked take her to the doctor's office so he could hear firsthand what the doctor had to say about their baby. At first, Wicked was against going to the hospital with Meagan but Wicked saw how it had upset her, so he gave in and decided he'll go with her. Evil had just texted Wicked and told him that everybody was going to the concert tonight and that their Cincinnati Kats needed 125 bricks. Wicked told Evil that he would be tied up with Meagan at the hospital. Evil told Wicked not to sweat anything and that he would manage everything while Wicked went with Meagan to the hospital.

Wicked told Evil to call him and give him the latest update and be ready for the concert at eight tonight. It was already 1:30 in the afternoon and Meagan's appointment was at 3 o'clock. Wicked couldn't stand the smell of hospitals, especially after he had spent over two weeks in Grant for multiple gunshot wounds. The nurse finally called Meagan in, and she told Wicked to join her. Wicked listened as the doctor told Meagan that she had dilated four centimeters (about 1.57 in) and she will be due to have her baby within the next three to five days depending on how much more she dilates. The doctor told Meagan that he would see her in three days to see how much she had dilated. Doctor Hamed told Meagan to get plenty of rest because she was going to need it.

As they drove home, Meagan told Wicked that she didn't want him to go to that concert tonight because she has a bad feeling about tonight. Meagan went on to say "babe, you know I would never tell you not to go, especially knowing how much you have been planning and waiting on this, but I just got a terrible feeling about you being there with Evil and the gang." Wicked seeing how shaken up his girl was, did everything in his power to ease her mind, but Meagan was adamant about this and started crying. Wicked remained silent as they rode home. All he could think about was being at that concert, so Wicked thought to himself that he wouldn't go to the after-party. He would come home after the concert so Meagan would feel good that he was home unharmed. Wicked had made his mind up that as soon as Meagan recovered from the delivery of their baby, he was taking her to the Bahamas where she had always wanted to go. Wicked called Robyn to run those 25 bricks he has over there to his little cousin out west on Sullivan Ave. Robyn quickly made that run.

Wicked's phone was going crazy, and he couldn't seem to answer it fast enough. Evil was trying to tell Wicked that the play with Cincinnati was a success and Robyn was trying to tell Wicked that her run was a success as well. There were so many people calling Wicked to make sure he was going to be at the concert that it was driving him crazy. Wicked had just turned the radio on and to his surprise, he heard the man on the radio say, "Our home grown rap star Wicked will be the opening act for Lil Boosie tonight at the VALLY DALE, so everybody show up and show your support." At first Wicked thought he was high, but he hasn't smoked shit since he has been with Meagan all day. He knew he couldn't smoke around her. So, he called his man who was producing his mix tape and asked him what the fuck was that all about? Million-dollar Meech told Wicked that his people reached out to Lil Boosie's camp, and I explained to them how you were doing crazy numbers just in this alone and it would be a win for you to open for Lil Boosie. Million Dollar Meech has a reputation that was gold or should I say platinum. So, he convinced Lil Boosie's people to set the shit in motion. Wicked was speechless on the other end of the phone as he listened to his producer explain to him what was going on! Wicked said fuck it, I'm doing this for Ohio. It was a little after 6 pm and Wicked called Robyn and explained to her to have Selina and Boo get all his dancers and artists ready to perform on this big stage ASAP. Wicked called Meagan and explained to her what was going down. She had mixed emotions but told her man that she loved him and to be safe. Wicked needed to hear that from his girl because he has big plans for her after the baby. Wicked hurried to Valley Dale where everyone was already waiting for him. He saw Lil Boosie and then Kodak Black and they met and spoke briefly. Lil Boosie looked at Wicked and asked Wicked if he knew the verses to his song "Emotionally Scarred" because he wanted Wicked to go bar for bar, and verse for verse with him on stage to give his hometown something to remember for a lifetime. Wicked said hell yeah let's do it.

As the crowd made its way into the club, Wicked estimated it had to be at least ten thousand people out there and he was ready to flow. Wicked came out on Q and rocked the crowd with his hit single "Real Street Nigga" and a couple more tracks from his mix tape. Then Kodak Black took the stage and rocked the bitch and Lil Boosie went out there with him. Then as Lil Boosie was performing his hit song "Set It Off," Wicked came on the stage and Lil Boosie looked at Wicked and said make these muthafuckas give you a standing ovation. Then Lil Boosie started the hook for that song and Lil Boosie and Wicked made history together. Gucci performed as a guest rapper and shut the club down after he did about five songs. The concert was legendary and Wicked became street and rap certified in everybody's eyes. The after-party was sure to be a hit because everybody was going to Downtown Dolls. Evil, who was loving every moment of his niggas success finally caught up with Wicked, hugged his brother, and said Wicked you did it my nigga you set the city on fire. Wicked assured Evil that they would sit down and discuss their next move because they both knew that all the bricks were gone, and they had to give Hector and Louis over three million dollars. But the money wasn't a problem because they knew that they had made over thirty million dollars since their return from Miami. All Wicked wanted to do was to party like it was 1999 and enjoy his friends and family. Wicked has totally forgotten that he had given Meagan his word that he wasn't going to the after-party, but he thought to himself how can I not go? So, off to Downtown Dolls it was, and he wasn't about to let nothing, or nobody ruin this night for him.

Damn, Wicked thought as he was amazed at how many people could fit in this place. He has never been here, but people talked about this spot a lot. Because it was downtown, a lot of people stayed away from here because the police would shut this bitch down in a heartbeat. Wicked was feeling the love and everybody was showing love. Wicked had his back turned from the D. J's booth and this lil redbone named Toyia spoke to him and asked if she could holla at him. Wicked asked her who she was with because he knew she was from the southside of Columbus, and he didn't get along with them too well. Rumor has it that the niggas shot his brother Willis, but Wicked had fucked Toyia's lil fine ass a few times in the past. He hasn't seen her in a while so, as they were small-talking, old boy walked up and said, "Wicked you are tripping with that one homie," Toyia said, "James you are tripping for real."

Wicked couldn't believe what he was hearing. This James kat was tripping hard about this bitch that Wicked hasn't seen in months. James started going crazy and started getting louder and louder creating a show like a clown. Wicked looked at Toyia and said please take your man and y'all go have a drink or two on me. Wicked gave her a hundred-dollar bill, but Toyia said "Wicked that isn't my man I don't fuck with him." She went on to finish by saying that I haven't messed with that clown since last year, so he was on some bullshit." It was at that very moment that Wicked realized that James was hating on him for God knows why.

Evil had heard the two men arguing and knew that he had to get Wicked away from that scene before things get out of hand. Just as Evil walked over there to calm the situation down, James' boyz came running over there talking about what y'all bitches on. Wicked and Evil both told them dudes that they didn't want any trouble and that it was a misunderstanding. However, the Columbus police had come to the scene and told everybody that none of this would be tolerated, or somebody was going to jail.

Wicked assured the police that it was a misunderstanding that got out of control, but everything was good now. The nigga Wicked exchanged words with was telling Wicked that he didn't like him, and he would be waiting on Wicked outside in the parking lot to handle this shit. Evil asked Wicked if he knows the guy. Wicked told Evil that he has never seen that nigga before in his life. Most of the people in the club told Wicked that the dude had just gotten out of jail about a week ago. So, Wicked and Evil assumed this was some "broke as fuck" boy that was looking to make a name for himself. Nevertheless, the police had to escort James and his crew out of the club. The party continued for a couple more hours and finally, everything was ending. All Wicked could think about was getting home to Meagan and relaxing after this long-ass night. Everyone was pouring out of the club and going to their cars. Wicked and Evil were walking towards Evil's Porsche truck when an all-black Monte Carlo pulled up on the side of Evil's truck and the window rolled down slowly. Wicked had spotted the car creeping and had told Evil to look up. So, by the time the Monte Carlo pulled up beside Evil's truck Wicked and Evil had moved to the opposite side of the truck. The Monte Carlo slowed down and the same fuck boy that Wicked had been in an argument with in the club was leaning out the window with a Glock nine in his hand shouting, "You a dead nigga Wicked" and let off about six to seven rounds. All the bullets missed Evil and Wicked, but Wicked had sent Robyn outside during the commotion and snuck out of the club and grabbed Wicked's nickel plated 357 autos. So, nobody saw Robyn hand Wicked the gun outside because there were so many people in the parking lot so it was impossible to have noticed it. Wicked leaped from the ground with his adrenaline running and fired back at the Monte Carlo as it sped off and crashed into a utility pole. Wicked and Evil jumped into Evil's Porsche truck and fled the scene as well.

Shortly thereafter, Wicked's phone vibrated, and it was Robyn on the other end telling Wicked that James had been shot in the neck twice and she heard somebody say that nigga was slumped over out the window of that Monte Carlo dead than a muthafucker. Wicked's heart sank, and Evil could tell by the look on Wicked's face that something was wrong. Evil asked his bro what was up and Wicked said "man Robyn just said that bitch ass nigga is dead." Evil couldn't believe what he had just heard and was shocked. Evil drove for the next 45 minutes in complete silence. Neither Wicked nor Evil had anything to say as both men tried to wrap their minds around what the fuck had just happened. Wicked, quickly thought about what Meagan had been saying to him all day. Wicked kept replaying those infamous words in his head repeatedly. "Wicked please don't go, stay home babe I got a bad feeling about tonight." Wicked's whole life flashed before his eyes. As Evil pulled into Wicked's driveway, all Wicked could think about was how he was going to tell Meagan what just happened.

Chapter 3:

Deal or No Deal?

The words hit Meagan like a ton of bricks and Wicked tried to explain the events to her as they occurred. Her heart felt like it was going to explode inside her chest. Wicked stood in front of his baby momma and almost cried himself as he watched Meagan cry like she had just lost her father all over again. The pain was too unbearable for Meagan to endure, and her mind could not process the thought of her losing her man for anything. As the room began to spin and Meagan looked around and saw everybody talking, she couldn't hear any words coming out of their mouths. Meagan began to feel weak, and her body collapsed in the middle of the living room. Wicked rushed to her side. As Wicked tried to help Meagan to her feet, it was Robyn's little brother who said

Wicked, look Meagan's pants is soaking wet. At that moment everyone in the room knew that Meagan's water broke. Evil called 911 and told Wicked to get the car. Wicked pulled to the front door in the Maserati and Evil and Robyn's lil brother helped Meagan to the car. Wicked told everyone to meet him at the hospital.

The doctor seemed to take forever before letting Wicked know what was going on with his baby's mom and his little girl. Finally, after what seemed to be ten hours, which was actually one hour, the nurse who Wicked remembered from Meagan's doctor's appointment told Wicked that Meagan was doing fine and that she had lost consciousness due to going into a state of shock. Wicked knew what had caused Meagan to go into shock, but he wasn't about to let this nurse or anybody for that matter know why Meagan fainted. The nurse told Wicked that Meagan was incredibly lucky because the baby was ok, but the doctor said that they were going to induce Meagan into labor so she would have to stay in the hospital. The news was bittersweet for Wicked because he knew it was his fault and his girl was in that condition because of him. He was relieved that the two people he loved the most were going to be ok. Wicked told Evil that he wasn't leaving Meagan's side and asked him to tell Robyn and Selina to get everything together. He asked him to call

Cleveland and get everyone down there on the same page. Robyn whispered to Wicked and told her nigga she would be there for him no matter what. Wicked kissed her on the cheek and said thanks! A few hours passed, and Meagan finally woke up. The first person she saw was her man, and that made her feel good. Meagan looked at Wicked and smiled and said, "Hey babe I Love You."

Wicked looked at his girl and said Meagan I Love You more than anything in the world and I mean that. Meagan stuck her hand out and Wicked reached out and held it tightly and the two of them just held hands for a moment. Wicked kissed her on the forehead and told her to get some rest so she could have her strength for their baby girl on the way. They both smiled at each other, and Meagan passed out. Wicked made multiple phone calls asking the number one question on his mind, have y'all heard anything from the streets? Evil told Wicked that he heard people in the street talking shit like that nigga Wicked shot Big Tone's little brother. Big Tone was one of Wicked's north-side older homies that he and his brother Willis used to rock with. Wicked didn't know his little brother James. After doing his homework, Wicked found out James was a young dope fiend type that has always been in and out of DYS and had just gotten out of Noble Corr. Now, Wicked's mind was racing because he knew that somebody was going to be running their mouth and sooner than later, the police would hear his name being involved in that shooting. The whole city was buzzing about that shooting mainly because it happened on the night of the concert. Plus, it just was a fucked-up timing. Wicked sat in the hospital room watching Meagan sleep and wondering what had gone wrong. All Wicked kept saying to his circle was "how the fuck did I go from a high to a low like this?" A nurse walked into the room and said to Mr. Jones, "I must wake your wife up to check to see if the medication made her dilate any closer to having this baby. As the nurse woke Meagan up, she saw Wicked was still there with her and she felt a sense of calmness fill her body and she was at peace. The nurse put on the latex gloves and began to perform several tests. Once the nurse had completed the test, she told Meagan that she had dilated four more centimeters and she was ready to give birth to her first baby. Wicked was so excited that he called everyone he could think of telling them to hurry to the hospital because Meagan was about to have the baby. Within minutes, it must have been over a hundred friends and family members there including Meagan's mother who had gotten to Columbus earlier that day.

The lobby in the hospital was crowded and everybody was waiting for the news to hear the baby's name, weight, etc. Meagan's mother was a nervous wreck and Wicked's mother along with everyone else were trying to calm her down. As they made efforts to ensure that Cynthia (Meagan's Mother) was calm, a nurse came from the delivery room removing her hat and gloves. The nurse had a huge smile on her face as she approached the crowd and said the mother and beautiful baby girl are doing fine and I'll send the proud father out to tell you guys her name and weight. As the nurse was leaving, she turned towards Meagan and Wicked's mothers and said, "congratulations." Wicked came out into the lobby about five minutes later happy as can be holding the Cuban cigars that the hospital had given him in his hands and passing them out to everyone. Wicked hugged his mom and then hugged Meagan's mom and said she weighed 7 lbs. 9oz (about 255.15 g). Everybody screamed at the same time asking Wicked what is the baby's name. Wicked smiled and said her name is Mariah Amber Jones. Wicked and Meagan's mother both smiled and Cynthia told her future son-in-law that she loved that name, and that it was so pretty. Now, it was Evil's turn to hug his partner and congratulate him on having a healthy beautiful baby girl. Wicked was feeling the love from all his family and friends. Wicked was called back to the delivery room because Meagan was asking for him. He walked into the room and saw Meagan holding their baby girl. She said to Wicked, "we did it baby, and now look what God gave us." Meagan was extremely happy she could finally tell Wicked what she had been wanting to tell him since she first found out that she was pregnant. She looked Wicked in his eyes and said Demetrious (Wicked's real name), I want to get married! Wicked looked at Meagan and said, "baby do you realize what you're saying?" Meagan became angry and said, "Wicked, listen to me and listen well. I know you're a street nigga and I know the shit you do in the streets from the bitches to the money. But now this baby has made you a father and it's time for you to become a real man." Meagan was so angry that Wicked had to tell her to calm down. Wicked has never seen Meagan that upset before. As he looked at Meagan holding his baby girl, he knew for the first time that life wasn't just about him anymore. The doctor who had delivered the baby told Meagan that everything went well with the baby and that Meagan would be free to leave in a couple of days. The nurse told Wicked and Meagan that they had to move the baby to the room where the family could see her. Cynthia and Tina (Wicked's mother) stood outside the window looking at their grandbaby with so much pride and their eyes started to water up. Wicked was sitting in the lobby shaking everybody's hands as the few people that had stayed at the hospital were leaving. Once everyone left, Wicked sat in the lobby with his mother, Meagan's mother, and Evil. Wicked sat and listened to the two older women express the importance of Wicked understanding that he has a huge responsibility now and that Meagan was going to really need him to be there for her and the baby. Wicked listened to the women and only wondered what was going to be their reaction once they found out about the shooting and he was the shooter! Wicked and his mother and mother-in-law went back to the room with Meagan, and they said their goodbyes and told Meagan that they all would be back in the morning. Everyone went to Wicked, and Meagan's house and they just sat around drinking and reminiscing. Wicked and Evil both knew that they had a severe problem on their hands that had to be dealt with. Just as Wicked suspected, his phone vibrated and Selina was on the other end telling Wicked that her girl Tasha knew James. She said that the nigga was telling people that he was going to rob Evil because Evil fucked his girl while he was locked up.

Wicked sat and thought for a minute and said to Selina find that bitch Evil fucked and get back to me. Wicked tapped Evil on the shoulder and nodded for him to go to the other room. Evil denied ever knowing James or the mystery bitch he was supposed to have fucked. Wicked was furious at Evil's behavior with them nothing ass bitches he loves to fuck with. Wicked told Evil that it was his loose dick that got him in this predicament. Evil knew Wicked was angry and had every right to be. He was concerned that his lifelong friend was thinking this situation was a result of him fucking some nothing-ass bitch. He knew deep down inside that he has a bad habit of fucking with bitches just because they have a big ass or a nasty walk.

Evil remembered the last time he fucked Tawana. He knows that she has a man that was locked up because Evil took pleasure in fucking her from the back while she talked to her nigga on the phone. Evil used to always tell Tawana to put the phone on speakerphone so he could laugh at the corny shit the nigga would say on the phone from the joint. But now the reality has set in and that bitch Tawana was in fact the nigga James girl. Evil remembered the tramp stamp on her lower back that said, "ENTER AT YOUR OWN RISK." He remembered laughing at the name that was under that saying. Evil bit down on his teeth because he now could see the name on Tawana's lower back from Nutting on that name that read JAMES.

Wicked couldn't believe the chain of events that unfolded. All he kept saying to himself was, I got to figure this shit out because I can't leave Meagan and my baby girl out here alone. It had gotten late so Wicked had told Meagan's mom and his mom to spend the night and they would all go see Meagan in the morning. Wicked tossed and turned all night thinking about the shooting. The next morning Meagan was wide awake breast-feeding little Mariah when the news came on the hospital's TV, and she couldn't believe her eyes. The news reporter was talking about the shooting that appeared to be gang-related that happened at the Downtown Dolls, where Wicked had the after-party at. As the reporter continued to speak about the shooting that left one man dead, the news showed Wicked and Evil as suspects. Meagan at once called Wicked and asked him what the news was talking about. Just as Meagan was informing Wicked of what the news had said, Wicked's mother and Meagan's mother came to Wicked's bedroom and stood at the doorway, and said have you seen the news? Wicked said, "no I haven't but Meagan is on the phone right now telling me about it." Wicked told Meagan he would be there shortly and that she should not worry because it was a misunderstanding that would be straightened out. But it was too late for Meagan not to worry because she was far from a fool. Wicked called Evil and Evil said yeah Bruh I already heard. Evil was on his way to

Wicked's house to figure out what the two of them were going to do. Wicked drove his Range Rover to the hospital so his mother-in-law and his mother could fit. Evil followed. Once at the hospital, Wicked spoke briefly but firmly to the ladies in his life and assured them that he would figure out all this mess. When Wicked drove to Robyn's house, he was surprised to find most of his support crew waiting for him, thanks to Robyn's efforts. They were all trying to talk at the same time but Wicked told them to shut the fuck up and go one at a time. Robyn went first telling Wicked what she heard, and that the homicide has been asking about you and Evil's whereabouts. Everyone else in the house said the same thing. The bottom line was Wicked, and Evil had to figure out how in the fuck they were going to clear their names from this bullshit. Wicked decided that he was going out of town to clear his mind, Selina, and Robyn both said that they were going to be by Wicked's side no matter what and that they were going wherever Wicked went. Wicked tried to argue with them, but he knew it was a waste of time. Selina and Robyn always were good to Wicked, and they had his back.

Meagan just won his heart. The day was moving along and Wicked found himself looking in his rearview mirror with every move he made. This state of paranoia was making him sick to his stomach, and he knew he had to leave that town before he suffocated in his own paranoia. Meagan couldn't believe that Wicked was a possible suspect for murder. She kept asking her mother and Wicked's mother how this could be happening to us. Meagan's heart was so heavy with fear and the sickening feeling that her man could go to prison! Meagan had called her mother earlier that week and asked her to come and be with her because she was scared about having her first baby. Plus, Meagan knew that she was going to tell Wicked that she wanted to get married, and she wanted her mother by her side. So, Cynthia flew in from Atlanta to be by her daughter's side. Evil didn't know if he was coming or going. This was his first time ever being involved in any type of street drama, especially some real live gangster shit. Evil quickly realized that Wicked has always been the one that handled all the violent shit in the streets. Evil kept saying to Ashley that he didn't pull the trigger and he didn't even have a gun. Now it was Evil's girl who was crying and upset that her man was a suspect in a murder case. Ashley knew that Evil could go to prison, and she was scared for her and her two-year-old daughter.

Evil contemplated his next move, and eventually decided to call Tawana and see if he could get some info from her about this James nigga. Who did he run with? Evil picked Tawana up and they drove out to Blacklick to a spot Evil has out there. Tawana swore to her dead father that she didn't know James was coming after him. Tawana did admit that she told James about Evil because Kats from Cleveland Ave had seen Evil's Chevelle leaving Tawana's spot a few times. So, word had gotten back to James that Tawana was fucking with someone named Evil. But Evil's name didn't ring a bell like Wicked's name did, so James found out that Evil was Wicked's right-hand man and decided to go after the stronger of the two. Tawana claims she didn't even talk to James since he got out. As Evil was dropping Tawana off, Ashley called him and said that two detectives had just left their house looking for him. Armed with this information, Evil dropped Tawana off and texted Wicked, and gave him the information he had just received. Wicked read the text and told Robyn and Selina to get the plane tickets for Miami ASAP. Wicked knew that leaving Meagan right now was the hardest thing he ever had to do but he had to get his mind clear. Wicked called Hector and told him everything and Hector told Wicked not to worry and that it would work itself out. Evil couldn't go home so he had Ashley and their baby girl meet him in Cleveland. Ashley told Evil that she wasn't running from the police because she knew she could get in trouble. Ashley wanted Evil to tell the detectives that he didn't pull the trigger and he didn't have a gun. Evil knew what Ashley was asking him to do was snitch on his brother and he would never do that. Meagan was furious and cussed the detectives out as they repeatedly asked her in front of her mother and Wicked's mother about hangouts and who he was with. Meagan would never, ever give Wicked to the police or anybody for that matter. The detectives left their cards and told Meagan it would be in her best interest to call them once she heard anything about Wicked. The buzz was all over Columbus that Wicked and Evil were wanted for the murder of James Patterson. It was 9 pm when the plane landed in Miami and Wicked knew this was far from a vacation. As Wicked, Robyn, and Selina walked to their hotel rooms, Wicked told his thoroughbreds that he appreciated them more than they could imagine. They both looked at Wicked and said at the same time, "Remember you taught us that Loyalty is Royalty so that's what it is with us."

Wicked smiled because he knew he had schooled them well. Over the next two weeks, Wicked didn't talk to anyone outside of Miami except Meagan and he told her what to tell Evil who was lying low in Houston, Texas. Wicked knew he couldn't call Evil because he knew the police would be all over him. Evil knew that Wicked would be on fire as well. So, they both decided to communicate underground. Wicked had really begun to miss his baby girl and Meagan so he decided to fly them to Miami. Meagan was terrified that Wicked was living like a fugitive at large and she told him that she kept having these bad dreams that the police shot and killed him in the streets. Meagan started to share with Wicked how they were being constantly harassed by the police. They were searching their homes and even went to Wicked's mother's workplace to harass her. Meagan told Wicked that she was going to move to Atlanta with her mother until this stuff got straightened out. Wicked knew he had to save his family. It was at that moment that he decided to get the best lawyers money could buy and fight this shit head-on. Wicked told Meagan, Selina, and Robyn that he was going to play the self-defense strategy. Everybody was ok with the idea and Meagan believed in her man's ability to make something shake. Evil was asking Wicked if he was sure this was the angle that they would play. Wicked assured Evil that this was their best chance to beat this shit and he was tired of running. They met with the Orlosky Law Firm, and they told Wicked and Evil not to talk to anybody, not even their girlfriends or wives. Dan Orlosky was the best trial lawyer in Columbus and was listed as the fifth best in Ohio. Wicked's mother had gotten in contact with this law firm through her husband who had them thirteen years ago when he beat that

R.I.C.O. charges the government had put on him. As they got to the police station and were met by the homicide detective, Wicked, and Evil were separated. Several minutes went by and both were processed and fingerprinted. Wicked was the first to be brought downstairs where his $250,000 bond had been posted.

Twenty minutes later Evil was joining Wicked in the parking lot as the two men were free on a quarter-million-dollar bond courtesy of the Orlosky Law Firm. Wicked and Evil sat in their lawyer's office as Dan Orlosky explained to them what exactly was going on. Mr. Orlosky was all over the evidence that the D.A. had and what the D.A. was planning to use against his clients. The D.A.'s office painted a picture that represented Mr. Jones aka Wicked as the trigger man and Mr. Smith aka Evil as the accomplice who drove the getaway car. Even though Wicked and Evil knew that's not how the shit went down for some strange reason people in the streets were hating Wicked. Or was it just Wicked that people were hating on? Let's be honest gentlemen, Mr. Orlosky said in a calm manner. What we have here is a war of words. We have a group of people saying this and a group of people saying that. The bottom line is simple, Mr. Jones you got gun residue on your clothes that came from the same gun that fired the fatal shot that killed Mr. Patterson and that's the problem! Wicked, knowing where this was going, asked his lawyer what was the worst- and best-case scenario. Mr. Orlosky said, "Well to be honest in your situation with a brand-new baby and a pretty wife everybody loses in those scenarios. I will say this, the D.A. is pushing second-degree murder and that's twenty years before parole. However, you're eighteen years old with a new baby and no priors, I'm quite sure I can get this dropped down to involuntary manslaughter and you out in ten. Wicked looked at Meagan as she burst out in tears wishing she wasn't in the room right now. Wicked's mother also was visibly shaken that her son might be going to prison for 10 long years. Evil finally spoke up and said to Mr. Orlosky, can we pay more money to get this shit thrown out? Mr. Orlosky said let me be perfectly clear, I have already received over one hundred and fifty thousand dollars to stand for you and Mr. Jones so believe me, money won't win this case. Wicked jumped at the opportunity to ask what it will take to win this case. Mr. Orlosky smiled and said common sense, my common sense. Mr. Orlosky advised Wicked and Evil to go home and get some sleep because they have to appear in court Thursday, so they have three days to decide what direction they wanted to pursue in this case. Mr. Orlosky told Wicked and Evil that he would handle that court date, but they had to let him know before Thursday what they want him to do. Evil sat on the couch as Ashley kept reminding him of what Mr. Orlosky said about common sense. Evil knew it was Wicked who had gotten a raw break and was charged as the shooter. He was only looking at two years for accessory to manslaughter.

Evil knew deep down that with a lawyer like Dan Orlosky he wouldn't spend a day in jail. Wicked paced back and forth as he listened to Meagan and his mother try to convince him that his options were slim to none if he took this case to trial. Especially with all the so-called witnesses the D.A. had ready to testify that they saw Wicked fire the shots out of the truck. Meagan was practically begging Wicked to strongly consider taking that 10-year deal. Even Wicked's mother was telling him that 10 years was better than twenty. And she was too old for him to be gone 20 years and still wasn't guaranteed to be paroled after 20 years. Wicked sat back and listened to what these two women were saying, but he wasn't trying to hear it, so he decided to take a ride. Wicked arrived at Robyn's house smelling like straight Henny and purp. Robyn knew that Wicked was stressing hard and she felt bad for him. Selina and Robyn's cousin Ashley came over to Robyn's because Wicked had told Selina to bring Ashley with her. Evil knocked on the door and Robyn let him in. Now, the old gang was together like in old times except this time things weren't so lovely. Wicked broke the silence and told Robyn to turn on some music to liven up the mood. Evil, seeing that Wicked wanted to take his mind off the case decided to break out his pills. Selina, the pill head told Evil to give her a pill to put in her pussy so she could fuck him and Wicked like a porn star. Evil who was a trick for a nasty bitch asked Selina if he could put the pill in her pussy? Robyn joined in as well as Ashley. Before you knew it everybody in the house was partying and Wicked took Robyn and Ashley to the back room with him leaving Selina and Evil alone. Evil made his move on Selina and pulled her jeans off and admired her red boy shorts that barely covered her ass. Selina was aware that Evil couldn't fuck so she knew she wasn't about to get any serious fucking.

Wicked had Robyn's ankles by her ears with her ass hanging off the king-size bed as he stood in front of her giving her nothing but dick. Ashley was riding Robyn's face and just as Robyn was about to cum, she said oh Wicked I'm about to cum on that dick. Wicked, knowing Robyn was a squirter pulled his dick out and allowed Robyn to spray him like a skunk would spray in the air. Ashley, not wanting to be outdone told Wicked to fuck her in the ass while she played with her clit. Wicked had his way and before long Ashley was squirting like a super soaker water gun. Then Wicked had both Robyn and Ashley suck his dick and he sprayed both of their faces with nuts everywhere. Early the next day, fresh from their triple x performance, all the women in the room started to laugh and make jokes about how Evil has a short but thick dick and the fact that he came super-fast. Evil, not wanting to be the butt of nobody's joke said fuck y'all. Y'all don't be complaining while I'm giving y'all this dick. Robyn said nigga I know you aren't talking after the last time I gave you some pussy and you said yes, I know Wicked don't hit it like this.

Robyn reminded Evil that while he was hitting it from the back, she had to tell him to smack her ass like Wicked was doing and go deeper and harder like Wicked was doing. Evil told Robyn she was full of shit just like Selina and Ashley. Wicked jumped to Evil's defense and said, "Hey y'all get off my boy's back." He then made a joke and said it isn't his fault that he got a little dick because his daddy cursed him. Everybody started laughing at that comment even Evil had to laugh but he was upset deep down at Wicked for siding with them bitches over him.

The crew continued to hang out the rest of the day trying to make light of Wicked and Evil's court date in a couple of days. Later that evening Wicked sat with Meagan in their kitchen as she prepared his favorite meal. (Fried Chicken, Mac and Cheese, candied yams, mustard greens, and her famous German Chocolate Cake). Wicked sat and destroyed the food Meagan cooked him. Meagan asked Wicked what he was planning to do about his legal situation. Wicked said after a slight pause, "Babe, I'm going to take the deal and run. Wicked had thought long and hard and he knew that Dan Orlosky had told him the truth about being smart and using common sense. Plus, Wicked wasn't willing to roll the dice with his family on the line! Wicked and Meagan had sex at least ten times that night, and the next day. Wicked woke up Thursday morning and his lawyer was calling him telling him to meet him in his office in an hour. Wicked and Evil sat and listened to Dan Orlosky as he explained to them what he has done with their sentencing arraignments. Dan Orlosky told Evil since he didn't have any priors and he didn't pull the trigger; the D.A. was willing to give him five years' probation. Dan told Wicked that the best he could do for him was involuntary manslaughter which carried the ten-year max. Wicked looked at Evil and said fuck it I got to do what I got to do. Wicked stood up and shook Mr. Orlosky's hand and said thank you sir and what doesn't kill me will make me stronger. The courtroom was filled to the brim with people, giving off the impression that a VIP was in town. Dressed impeccably for the occasion, Wicked was surrounded by his entire family who were there to show their unwavering support. As the judge told the defendant to stand, Wicked turned and looked at Meagan, his daughter, and his mother. He silently told them that he loved them. All Wicked could remember was that old ass white man with silver hair looking at him saying "I sentence you to a term of ten years in prison at the Correction Reception Center and that the defendant is to be remanded in the custody of the Sheriff's Department for transport." There it was; Wicked has gotten ten years and was on his way to CRC to start his bid. The courtroom was silent as the sheriff handcuffed Wicked and took him through the back of the courtroom.

Chapter 4:

Growing Pains

Meagan confided in her mother about how difficult it had been for her since Wicked had been sent to prison and how it had turned her life upside down. They were sitting in the kitchen as she expressed her concerns to her mother. Cynthia tried to comfort her daughter by telling her that everything was going to be ok, but Meagan knew everything was not going to be ok. In fact, Meagan felt like she has been diagnosed with cancer and that her life was over. To Meagan Wicked was the air that she breathes, and now she felt as though she couldn't breathe anymore. However, Meagan kept rewinding the words in her mind that Wicked was saying to her as he was being led out of the courtroom, which was "Babe be strong and hold us down, because you are a trooper, and this is just a test!" Meagan knew that she didn't have a choice. She understood that life wasn't fair and that her man was going to need her more than ever now.

Evil had come over to check on Meagan and the baby as she talked to Wicked on the phone. Evil has been coming over every day and was a tremendous help to Meagan and the baby. Wicked had told Evil that he was glad to have Evil as a loyal friend in his life, especially now. Wicked and Meagan had come to an understanding that Meagan was going to move to Atlanta to be with her mother and family so she wouldn't be out there in Ohio alone. Wicked knew that Meagan would make sure she and her baby Mariah visit him at least once a month. Evil told Wicked not to worry about visits because if he had to, he would fly Meagan and the baby back and forth himself. Meagan realized that several months had gone by and the weather was starting to break, and April was warm. She had just come from seeing Wicked who just got out of the hole for getting caught with a cell phone. She earlier told Wicked that since the weather has gotten better, she was going to move to Atlanta. Meagan and Wicked decided that it was best for Meagan to sell the two homes they shared in Cleveland and Grove Port. Meagan's mother is a realtor so it was easy to market, and sell the houses.

Within a few weeks, Meagan was off to Atlanta to start her new life working with her mother in the real estate market. Wicked, fresh out of the hole for fighting was talking to Corey (Robyn's little brother) on the newest Galaxy 15 cell phone. Wicked told Corey that he was trying to transfer from Lebanon and get to Ross so he could be closer to Columbus. Corey has been doing everything for Wicked since Evil was busy running in and out of town so much. Corey has always been Wicked's extra eyes and ears in the streets before his case. He knew that Corey was somebody he could trust with his life. Wicked wasn't adjusting well to prison life. In fact, Wicked has been to segregation at least twenty times during the first six months of being in Lebanon. On Wicked's very first day at CRC, he got into a fight because a nigga called him a bitch and Wicked tried to break his jaw.

Shortly after he got out of the hole for that, he was in a cell with some old head named S.T. who knew Wicked's pop and gave him the first cell phone he got caught with. Young Wicked had it in his mind that he was going to do the time and the time wasn't going to do him. He enjoyed getting visits, especially when Meagan and his daughter came to see him. Wicked had grown his dreads back so when Meagan came to see him during the last visit, she was shocked that Wicked's hair has grown so much. Today was Friday and Evil popped up on a surprise visit and Wicked was happy to see his nigga. Evil looked good and always had on the newest gear. Evil told Wicked that everyone was doing well and that his mother has finally gone to rehab. Wicked was happy Evil's mother went to rehab because he knew how much that affected Evil, growing up and seeing his mother smoke crack like she did. Evil was keeping it one thousand with Wicked since Wicked has been gone and Wicked knew Evil was missing him just as much as Wicked was missing him. The two men hugged, and Evil told Wicked he would be back in a few weeks after he came from Miami.

Meagan was quickly making a name for herself as a new young realtor in Atlanta. She had built a reputation as a sharp-minded businesswoman who was selling house after house. Wellington's Realtors, the company Meagan worked for, had given her a raise just after her first year on the job. Meagan was given her own office in downtown Atlanta. Young Mariah looked more like her mother, but everybody knew that Mariah had her daddy's strong personality. Mariah now two years old, wasn't like most kids her age. She was already talking like a five-year-old and was able to read at a preschool level. Meagan loved Mariah but hated how her own mother would constantly spoil Mariah. Meagan and her mother would argue about Cynthia spoiling Mariah and Meagan would always tell her mother that she didn't want Mariah growing up thinking and feeling like she had to depend on somebody to do everything for her. Meagan taught Mariah how to be self-sufficient because Wicked would tell Meagan he never wants his daughter to depend on any man for her wants and needs.

Meagan received a call from a potential big client one morning, so she decided to dress for success. Little did she know that this day would change her life. Wicked had just been visited by his mother and two sisters. He has been locked up for two years now and has started to get his weight up from all the pull-ups, pushups, and dips he has been doing. Wicked hasn't been to the hole in over nine months now and while staying true to form, he just received a package from a CO that his lil bro Corey knew. Wicked was pushing the majority of the "loud" within the compound and everyone in Lebanon loved Wicked because he was the go-to man for whatever you wanted and needed. He was in his cell talking to Corey on his cell phone when Corey told him he had heard that one of Evil's safe houses had gotten hit for four hundred and fifty bricks. Wicked was telling Corey how he felt that Evil had to start setting an example for these clowns in the street. Corey told Wicked that he and his young gunners could and would handle that shit for Evil. Wicked told Corey to get it done and let him know when it was done. Wicked called Selina who was still handling shit for him like meeting COs and picking up money. He just found out that his sister's boyfriend had gotten killed in Cleveland. Wicked was cool with his sister's boyfriend but he had told him to slow down because his name was ringing heavily in the streets. But like most street niggas, Mike wasn't hearing what people were telling him and now he is dead. Wicked told Selina to make sure she and Robyn were careful and let Corey know what they needed, and he would handle it off Wicked's word. Selina told Wicked she was coming to visit him this Saturday so she could give him some pussy. Wicked has his nigga who worked in the visiting room. He would have the CO leave him and Selina in the bathroom for ten minutes for five hundred.

Evil was so frustrated at Ashley because all she kept doing since he had just taken a loss was complain about him running the streets like he was still chasing Wicked like a lost puppy. Evil was so tired of putting up with Ashley's mouth that he was going to leave her and be done with their relationship. Ashley is so manipulating and conniving. She responded by saying "Yeah, you walk out that door but remember this on your way out; your boy Wicked tried to fuck and your ass was too stupid to see it!" Evil looked at her and said bitch you are lying, and you did fuck him! Corey sat and listened to Evil talk about what Ashley had told him about Wicked and that he believed Wicked did try to fuck Ashley. Corey told Evil that he was crazy, and he knew that Wicked was loyal to Evil to ever play him like that. Evil's mind was racing as he contemplated his next move.

Meagan, ready for her big day on the job arrived at the rental site where she would be showing her potential buyer the property. As she waited for her buyer to arrive, she got a call from her boss who reminded her to do whatever she had to do to land this potential buyer. See what Meagan did not realize was that the potential buyer she was about to meet was Antonio Simpson, a first round draft pick of the Atlanta Hawks. Antonio Simpson and his agent arrived, and Meagan met the two men. As Meagan began to show the gentlemen the house, she noticed that Antonio is extremely handsome. Meagan offered the men something to drink and at that moment Antonio said to Meagan, I see you're not wearing a wedding ring. Meagan who was taken by total surprise responded, "no I'm not married."

Meagan sat in her bathtub and sipped a glass of wine she had poured herself as she thought about how her relationship with Antonio had blossomed. As Meagan sipped the wine, she thought of Wicked and how much she missed the father of her child. Antonio was completely different from Wicked; he is a momma's boy and this drove Meagan insane. Meagan could never understand how a grown-ass man would still depend on his momma the way Antonio did. Antonio would call Meagan every day and send flowers to her job. Of course, this led to her being the most hated female in the company where she worked. Meagan remembered their first encounter when she sold him the home that they had sex in. It was an awkward experience for Meagan because Antonio is this big-time athlete, but Meagan didn't know who he was. Antonio loved the fact that Meagan didn't know who he was or hardly anything about basketball. Meagan always said to herself that if Antonio wanted to know how to cook cocaine or roll a blunt, she was his girl. The thought that Meagan had fallen for somebody like Antonio proved to her that she really loved Wicked and missed him dearly. Antonio was gone a lot due to the basketball season off and running. So, Meagan and Antonio only saw each other when the Atlanta Hawks played at home. Even at some of his home games, they didn't spend too much time together for several reasons. Meagan couldn't believe she has been dating Antonio for over two years now. Meagan's phone rang while she was at her mother's house. She looked at the caller ID and saw that it was Wicked calling. She answered the phone and Wicked asked her why she hadn't seen him in almost two years. Meagan really couldn't face Wicked and tell him that she was seeing Antonio. Wicked was her first and only love. Hell, Wicked had broken her virginity when she was fourteen. Meagan assured Wicked that she was taking some vacation time from her job and would fly to see him in a couple of weeks.

Corey had just left Evil's bar when he texted Wicked and told him that it was true Meagan was involved with some basketball player that played for the Atlanta Hawks. Wicked asked Corey if Evil knew, and Corey told him that everyone found out through ESPN. Wicked told Corey that he was pissed at Evil because, after all these years, he was still playing captain save a hoe. For the first time in Wicked's life, he really felt hurt and betrayed by Meagan. And Evil, not wanting to argue or fall out with his lifelong friend sat at the bar of his own club and decided to confront Wicked about what Ashley had told him two years ago. Evil had always looked at Wicked as a big brother even though Evil was slightly older than Wicked. Nevertheless, Evil never really knew his own father but heard through rumor Ville that his father was a bitch ass clown and Evil never claimed the man that use to beat his mother as his father. As far as Evil was concerned, Big Moose was the only father figure he knew and respected. Wicked has been locked up a little over three years now and he has gotten the swing of doing time. Wicked would listen to the jailhouse lawyers as they constantly told him how the laws change all the time, and that Wicked could file for judicial release after he did five years. Wicked would always tell Evil that he wanted to shoot his shot at that judicial release. Evil was doing exceptionally well for himself, and he felt like he owed it all to Wicked. Evil has opened a successful nightclub and called it Miracles after his own daughter. Since Wicked had been gone, Evil kept the connection going with Hector and Louis. Evil gave Hector and Louis over three million dollars when Wicked left to pay their tab on the 250 bricks they had gotten in '2016. Evil told himself he wasn't taken any prisoners. The visiting room wasn't that crowded, and Meagan was looking good as usual. Wicked to her surprise was looking too damn fine. His hair is long, and his dreads hit his shoulders. Wicked had put on twenty pounds of muscle and he knew that Meagan was feeling him, but Wicked had to ask the million-dollar question. Do you love Ol' Boy? Meagan looked at Wicked and said no I don't love him, but I like him a lot. Now it was Meagan's turn to ask a question and she asked Wicked will you marry me if I leave him alone and wait for you? Wicked hesitated and said "Meagan, why do you want me to deal or think about it in here?" Meagan wasn't letting up this time and she asked again, "Will you marry me if I leave him alone?" Wicked said "I'll marry you when I get out. I'll give you the biggest, and baddest wedding that money can buy." Meagan said, "Wicked you're full of shit, and you just can't accept the fact that another nigga is hitting this pussy. Look how long I accepted your bitches!"

Wicked and Evil sat across from each other, neither man wanted to be the one to speak first. Evil broke the silence and asked Wicked what the fuck is the deal with Ashley? Evil hasn't spoken to Wicked in over six months, and Wicked had Corey convince Evil to see him. The two of them were in the visiting room and they couldn't believe that a bitch like Ashley had come between them. Ashley is someone Wicked had met before he even knew Evil. As a matter of fact, it was Wicked and Meagan who introduced Ashley to Evil. Wicked had warned Evil back then that Ashley was a party animal, and to be careful with her. However, Evil got Ashley pregnant after the first time he fucked her. Ever since Ashley had Evil's little girl, it was all she wrote. Ashley has Evil wrapped around her pinky finger. Nevertheless, Wicked had just explained to his best friend how it was Ashley that had tried to give him some pussy when Evil went to Cincinnati. Wicked told Evil that Ashley had gotten butt ass naked in their house, and Wicked had in fact checked her that night. He told Ashley that she should never ever play her hand like that again, or he would kick her ass himself. Evil knew Wicked wasn't lying and he was glad that he and Wicked finally talked about this. Both men shook hands and hugged, Evil told Wicked that Dan Orlosky was filing for his judicial release next month. Wicked has a new judge who was hard on violent crimes, and Dan Orlosky told Wicked over the phone that he wasn't sure how this judge was going to act about his judicial release. Wicked got the news as Ericka, Mr. Orlosky's secretary, explained to him that the judge denied his request for judicial release. Wicked took the news hard and swore that his next five years were going to be dedicated to his education. He was determined to better himself in every area of his life. Corey told Wicked that Robyn had just given birth to her second baby since Wicked had been gone. Wicked has not seen Robyn in three years and he knew that she was messing with some goon from Chicago. Lately, Selina hasn't been around much. It's been eighteen months since Wicked last saw her, and he knew that being in prison would reveal who would stick by him in the long run. Corey has grown up since Wicked had been gone. Corey was twenty years old now and was making serious moves in the streets. Evil didn't even know that Corey handled business at least twice for Evil who he had beef with. Corey had been Wicked's lil' bro since day one and Corey knew that he must prove to Wicked that he was that go-to person now. Everything Corey did was just the way Wicked did it. Wicked and Corey talked all the time and Corey had listened to Wicked and sat on the five bricks that he had because the drought was about to hit hard. Wicked heard that Hector and Louis had gotten killed in a Mexican Cartel turf war. Shortly after that the DEA and FBI had been popping shit all around the country. All over everyone was feeling the effects of these major drug raids. Homies would pull up on Wicked and tell him stories of Evil, and how he was the man out there and was winning. Wicked has gotten used to all the new Kats that came in and told him stories of Evil. Wicked knew that after six and half years of being locked up, Evil was still flamboyant. Corey wasn't going the way he did, and Wicked felt good because that was his lil Homie. The summer was coming and Wicked was about to transfer to a level one prison where his pops was staying. Wicked has been locked up for seven years now and has exactly 32 months (about two and a half years) left. He just had a family visit and his daughter, now about to be seven, was talking her father's ears off. Mariah talked to her dad about everything from her mother to her school to her two front teeth falling out. Wicked loved his little girl more than life itself and he swore every night that once he got home, he would have her with him every day. Wicked's mother was doing ok, and she told Wicked that his brother Willis had gotten married and was living in D.C. Wicked had only spoken to Willis once since Willis had been home. Willis had embraced Islam while he was in the feds and married a Muslim woman once he got out. Willis had told Wicked that he was done with the street life, and he hoped that Wicked would be done with the street life as well. Wicked always loved family visits because everyone always had a story to tell. Wicked has seen how a lot of people lost focus on their dreams, and how life has been too much for them to handle so they just simply gave up.

Meagan got dressed and thought to herself that she was going to tell Antonio that she was upset that he has been spending hardly any time at home. Meagan knew that Antonio has been distant ever since she had miscarried. The miscarriage devastated Meagan because she thought something was wrong with her body. She knew that she has been stressing a lot thinking about Wicked. Meagan was six weeks pregnant when she got word from Evil that Wicked had bought her a five-carat engagement ring. That had really upset Meagan and she was mad at Wicked for not just leaving her alone. Meagan had written Wicked and told him that she had given him the opportunity to have her hand in marriage, but he chose to play hardball. So, it was her turn to give him a dose of his own medicine. When Meagan first heard about the engagement ring, she quickly called Wicked's mother and told her that Antonio had given her an engagement ring as well. Wicked's mother told Meagan to follow her heart and listen to her guts and whatever decision she made; she would still support her.

Antonio had made dinner reservations at Two Chain's new soul food spot near downtown Atlanta. Antonio knew Meagan loved this place and he knew he had been away for a while. Knowing that Meagan was upset with his past behavior, Antonio tried to make things better by buying Meagan an all-white Bentley GT convertible for her birthday. Meagan ordered her favorite prime rib and lobster tail combo and Antonio ordered stuffed shrimp with Lemon flavored scampi. They ate their meal as the jazz music echoed in the background. Antonio is a baller to the fullest and money was not a problem for him. After all, he did sign a four-year ninety-six-million-dollar deal with a twenty-million-dollar signing bonus. So, one thing was for sure, Meagan enjoyed the finer things in life. Meagan confronted Antonio about not being in her life since she had the miscarriage and she told Antonio that things had to change, or she would rather be in a relationship by herself. Antonio couldn't understand Meagan. He felt as though someone in Meagan's shoes should just sit back and enjoy the ride. What Antonio didn't know was that Meagan was from the streets and she had boss game. So, Meagan would always say to herself "This country ass nigga got me twisted if he thinks I'm going for his weak ass drag." Antonio swore to Meagan that he was going to be better to her and for her. Antonio has never experienced anyone like Meagan. The first time Antonio fucked Meagan; she made him cum in less than five minutes. Meagan was always mad after they fucked, because he didn't fuck like Wicked. Antonio fucked like a white boy, and she hated that. After the dinner, Antonio drove Meagan to their ranch-style home that he had bought through her real estate company and they fucked for five minutes. As Meagan sat back on the bed and watched Antonio sleep, she wondered what Wicked was doing. She thought how much she missed him spreading her ass cheeks and power fucking her like she was a ten-dollar hoe. Meagan fell asleep thinking about Wicked's dick.

Wicked has finally transferred to Lancaster, a level one prison where his pops was staying. Big Moose had a lot going on, but Wicked was already aware of what his pops was into. The two of them hit the ground running, and Wicked was soaking up game from his pops like a sponge for real. Wicked has gotten into college and was involved in damn near every program the prison had to offer. Big Moose was glad to see his son doing all the right things to better himself before he went back home. Wicked had promised his pops that before he went home that he would get his degree in business management, and Wicked worked hard at his schoolwork. Wicked had fallen in love with Lancaster's music program. This was the first time in a few years that Wicked would go to the music room and write music and perform at shows inside the prison. Big Moose has never heard his son rap in person, and he was impressed with his son's rap skills. Wicked was learning more about the business game and his professor knew that Wicked wanted to learn all he could. Wicked was determined to make his dream of becoming a successful businessperson a reality, and nothing was going to stand in his way. He had a clear vision and was driven by a personal mission to succeed.

Chapter 5:

Streets On Life Support

The drought had hit hard, and Evil was trying to figure out what his next move was going to be. Another one of Evil's spots had just got hit by some stick-up boys. This is the second stash house that Evil had that was hit back-to-back. Evil sat back and tried to figure out how he was getting hit like this. He recalled the first time he took a loss. On that note, some thugs tied his lil' chick up and hit him for four hundred and fifty bricks. Now evil suffered two losses back-to-back, and on both hits, he lost over six hundred racks and over two hundred bricks. Evil sat on his couch and thought about where he was going to find another connection. The streets were on life support, and nobody had any work. Corey called Evil and told him that he knew some Africans that had some good ass Heroin.

Wicked told Evil on their last visit that the heroin was coming back hard. Evil wasn't familiar with the heroin game and was hesitant about meeting the Africans Corey was talking about. But Evil saw how Corey was eating off that heroin and decided to meet the African muthafuckers. Evil and Corey sat down, and Evil told Corey that his mind was made up and he wasn't taking any more losses. Evil always remembered what Wicked said when they copped their first brick. Wicked had told Evil that he went to his Russian dudes and copped some ARs and AK 47s and some handguns and got his feet wet in the streets. Evil learned how to cut that heroin like a pro. He knew that the shit he had was able to take three so he could take fifty and turn them into one fifty. He took off on that heroin game and in less than ninety days, he banked up seven hundred thousand dollars. Corey and Evil had become close, and Corey would tell Wicked what was going on firsthand. Wicked would talk to Evil and Corey practically every day. Evil started hanging in Cleveland tuff because the Ricans he used to fuck with were loving the deals Evil was giving them on the heroin. Evil started spending more time with his chocolate piece Monique. Monique was just what Evil needed because she knew that he was soft-hearted, but Wicked is a killer. Monique constantly told Evil, "That he had to trust her because niggas need a gangster bitch that's gone ride and die with their nigga." Monique is a thoroughbred and a top-of-the-line hustler. Evil didn't know what he had in Monique, and she proved her loyalty to Evil one day. Evil had accidentally left two bricks of that raw at her spot and Monique flipped that shit three times and gave Evil four hundred and seventy-five racks. Evil couldn't believe that Monique was this thorough. Now that Evil has a gangster bitch on his side, he knew nothing can stop him. As soon as shit started going well, Evil got a call from his people in Columbus saying that they got hit for ninety bands, but they knew who did it. Evil told Monique, "I need to handle that shit in Columbus, and I would be back as soon as I'm through." Monique told Evil, "You're moving too fast. Just let me handle that lil shit." Evil looked at Monique and said, "Babe what the fuck are you going to do?" Monique said, "You just take a trip to Houston for a week or two, and don't worry your pretty lil face off."

Monique got some gunners that she knew from the projects down the way on Cleveland's east side together, and sent them to Newark, Ohio where he lives. He is the one that hit Evil's spot and was hanging out at this white bitch's house everybody called Peaches. Monique didn't have any problems finding out who these clowns were. She learned a long time ago that if a lame-ass clown thought he was about to get some pussy, he would give you his momma's social security number. So, she used her contacts in Columbus to trick these bitches out of the info she needed to find these lames. What Monique ultimately discovered was Evil would fuck these bitches in the streets and run his mouth. Bragging to them about all the money he had here and there, and little did Evil know that the bitches weren't after his dick but his money. Monique had her gunners wait and catch the three lames ass bitches that hit Evil's spot, and as soon as they hit the parking lot; six motorcycles rode past blasting.

Words traveled throughout Columbus and Cleveland all the way to Cincinnati how the bitches got gunned down in Newark. While Evil was still in Houston, Monique called him and urged him to check out the viral video on YouTube that everyone was talking about. Evil, knowing what Monique had done was loving her for now. Corey was in the blind about Monique pulling the streets. The streets were starving, and everyone was in attack mode. Only certain home boyz were eating. Evil was the man again and everybody knew it. He had homies from all over Ohio calling his phone and trying to place an order. Corey eventually found out that Monique had orchestrated that hit in Newark and was impressed with her. Evil was doing numbers and had shit on smash. Wicked was perfecting his business skills while talking to Evil on a visit when Evil told him that his mother was sick, and it wasn't looking good. Now it has gotten worse and she has been in the hospital for a week. The doctor said that she was in bad shape. Evil confided in his brother from another mother and told him everything about Monique. Wicked already knew what was going on and told Evil that homies in the joint hear shit before people in the street hear shit. Neither of them knew how this was possible, but it was a fact. Wicked was down to two years left and he was telling Evil how much he appreciated everything Evil had done for him and his family. Wicked was doing well and it was Wicked that kept telling Evil to stop being so flashy. Wicked knew the streets were dry. Hell, this has been one of the worst droughts in a long time. Wicked knew that Evil is a loyal friend. Evil has done everything under the sun for Wicked since he has been locked up. When Wicked got to CRC, Evil had put ten stacks on Wicked's books. Evil would tell Wicked to send him homies name to put money on their books and to send food and clothes boxes in their names too. Evil never stopped doing that. Even to this day, Evil would still tell Wicked to send him some people's info so he could send Wicked whatever he needed or wanted. Evil would make sure that little Mariah made it to see her dad every birthday and holiday.

Evil was determined to make sure that Wicked had the chance to see his daughter. He was willing to fly to Atlanta himself to get Mariah if he had to. Wicked was grateful for Evil's support and recognized him as his closest friend.

Wicked knew that Corey was a loyal friend as well, but nobody on the planet has been by Wicked's side longer than Evil. Wicked remembered when Evil found out about Antonio that Meagan was with and told Wicked that he would get him wacked! Wicked laughed at his friend's love for him. He knew time was on his side now. Evil was celebrating the grand opening of his bar and grill called Miracles. This spot was named after his daughter. Evil had just left his daughter because Ashley was fighting him for full custody rights. He couldn't believe that Ashley was tripping like she was. He gave her half of everything he had and then some, but for some reason, Ashley wanted to punish Evil by trying to keep their daughter away from him. Ashley has been heartbroken ever since she and Evil split up, and not to mention that Evil believed Wicked over her back then. Monique has been holding it down for Evil and she put some of the baddest bitches in Cleveland at the bar & grill Evil just opened. Monique kept Evil on his game, especially when it came to them ratchet ass bitches Evil was a sucker for. Monique started teaching Evil how to turn the tables on them bitches. She told Evil to have them bitches tell them about some lames, and where they keep their money or dope at. Evil would tell Monique what he had found out and she would have their bitch ass taken to the top by her girls. Evil finally realized that it was these bitches that controlled most homies. Meagan hasn't been back in Ohio for at least three years now. The death of Evil's mother had all the old gang reconnecting. Everybody showed up at the funeral. Evil was so surprised to see Robyn after such a long time that he almost didn't recognize her, especially with her bright red hair and two kids. Selina was there looking good and still talking shit, everybody was there except Wicked. Evil knew that Wicked was going to take it hard and the prison wouldn't let him attend the wake or view the body. Evil and Wicked talked about what they were going to do once Wicked got home. Meagan had come to visit Wicked while she was in Ohio, and they had a good visit.

The funeral made Meagan to realize just how much she missed her friends and family back in Ohio. Meagan was close to Evil's mother, and she was sad that Evil's mom had passed away. Meagan knew in her heart that something had to give in her relationship with Antonio. The situation between Meagan and Antonio hasn't gotten any better, and Meagan felt like the only difference between a professional athlete and a street thug was that a street thug cares about bitches and how they felt, but a professional athlete didn't care about the bitches! Meagan knew that she had to let Antonio know that she wasn't about to continue to be played like a fool by anyone. All Meagan kept thinking about was what the fuck Wicked would say if he knew she was allowing this corny-ass Antonio to play her like a fool. She constantly thought about Wicked and how much she missed him. Every time Mariah would say she wanted to see her daddy, Meagan could see how Antonio would start acting funny. But Meagan knew that all the little games that Antonio was playing were soon to be finished. Courtney, one of Meagan's white friends had called her one day and told her that Antonio was at this gym with a white girl all hugged up. Meagan has been getting all sorts of information about Antonio and his love for his white girls. The Atlanta Hawks were having a four-game home stand and Meagan knew this was an opportunity for Antonio to spend as much time as he wanted with her. Antonio had only been home once since the Hawks had been in town for a whole week. Meagan found out that most of the players on the team were having a birthday party for one of their teammates. The party was at a location Antonio had taken Meagan to when they first started dating. Meagan pulled up at the valet parking and entered the club from the rear. Not wanting to make a scene, she entered the dimly lit club and spotted Antonio hugged up with this big-chested, flat booty, blonde hair, blue-eyed pale looking white bitch. Meagan had to stop and gather herself from laughing at what she was looking at. As Meagan walked towards the table where Antonio was sitting, Antonio looked and saw Meagan approaching the table. Antonio's eyes were so big that everybody turned to see what Antonio was looking at. Just as Antonio tried to stand, Meagan said "Bitch please don't even waste your time or mine." Meagan looked at everyone sitting at the table and realized that all these black ass men had a white bitch with them. So, Meagan said to Antonio as he sat there looking like the bitch he was, "Antonio you aren't shit but a country ass momma's boy." She went on to say, "I see you chose this white bitch over me because you fuck like a white boy and y'all deserve each other." Meagan grabbed a glass of wine from the table and threw it in Antonio's face. As she walked away, Meagan turned around and grabbed her big round ass with both hands and made her cheeks bounce. Then told Antonio, "Take a good look because your little dick ass will never see this ass again."

Wicked couldn't do anything but laugh as Meagan sat in front of him with her arms crossed. Meagan had told Wicked what she did to Antonio at the club a few weeks ago. Meagan knew that Wicked was the man for her even after eight years that he's been gone. They were still in love. Wicked told Meagan that he was at an all-time low when Meagan had gotten pregnant. Six weeks later, Wicked felt better after she miscarried but felt bad for Meagan who lost her baby. He was happy that Meagan was back in his life and that she left Antonio's ass alone. Now all Wicked needed was his freedom. Evil had shit running up and down I-71 and 75 north and south. Evil couldn't believe how much money was in the heroin game. All Evil knew was that if anyone got in his way, he was so much a boss he would have his bitch down them. Corey even noticed the change in Evil, and he knew that it was Monique that had Evil thinking like a mob boss with this off-with-your-head attitude now. Corey was loving this new Evil because people in the streets thought twice now about fucking with him. However, street thugs were still out there in the streets lurking and waiting for Evil to slip. Words on the street was that Evil was waiting for a fresh batch of some fish scale. The streets haven't seen fish scale in at least two summers, and the word had gotten out that Evil had it and was about to flood the streets with the shit. This buzz traveled all the way to Lancaster. Wicked called Evil and told him that he has shit under control and that people always were going to run their mouths when it came to him.

Evil and Corey had joined forces and were getting money together. Wicked has constantly told them they needed to work together. Plus, they all knew the old saying "two heads are better than one." To Evil, Corey reminded him of a younger Wicked in so many ways. They both didn't hesitate to bust their guns. Neither of them was afraid to go to war with any hood, city, or country. Corey would always say, "I'll go to war against Bin Laden!" Evil loved the fact that young Corey has the heart of a lion. In fact, the streets nicknamed him "Crazy C." Corey was leaving Miracles one night and a car had blocked his '68 442 super sport in the lot and Corey couldn't get out. While ol' boy who was blocking Corey was on the dance floor, Corey had one of his homies push the other car onto the street. The homeboys' car got smacked by a semi and the semi never stopped. That was just one of many stunts that Corey did. If ol' boy was acting disrespectful towards a female that he was with, Corey would have his lil homie beat ol' boy with a belt to teach him some manners. Evil used to tell Corey all the time to chill with the stunts he liked pulling on people in public. Corey used to always tell Evil that he was too scared, and that he needed to loosen up and have fun. Evil felt like he had outgrown that part of life. Corey had all the bitches chasing him because he would tell them bitches how good he could suck pussy. Corey has a big sexual appetite and loved redbones. He would be seen leaving a spot with two to three redbones nearly every night. Evil told his homie his dick was going to fall off from all that fucking. Corey would always say give me a blunt and a bitch and life's great. Everyone knew Corey was the life of the party and enjoyed him acting silly.

Evil has started to get more focused on his business mind. He has been taking Wicked's advice on trying to get educated on the street game. Wicked told Evil on one of their visits that Evil should attend a community college and take a small business management course, and Evil did just that. He enrolled in a community college near downtown Cleveland. He started learning the corporate side of the game and was fascinated by what he was learning. Evil felt like he had the upper hand over the average thug in the street because they didn't know the difference between being rich and wealthy. This newfound love Evil had gotten had him feeling like a real live boss. Monique constantly reminded him "You can take thugs out of the ghetto, but you can't take the ghetto out of a thug." Evil knew Monique was just talking shit because she was the one who told Evil that he had to find a way to clean his money. One of the things being in that business class taught him was how to wash dirty money. Evil finally got his hands on that fish scale he has been waiting on. The only problem was, everyone was waiting to get their hands on the same shit. When that shit hit the streets, it took off like wildflowers. The streets were going crazy, and Evil sat back like he was an evil genius. He told Corey not to be mistaken because this cocaine money wasn't like heroin money. This is the foundation of the average street hustler, and Evil knew there were a lot of homies in the streets that still would rather push fish scale than Mexican tar all day. In fact, Evil told Corey that he would rather push cocaine instead of heroin, but the heroin money was off the charts. Most kat's in the street knew you could make anywhere from one hundred and fifty thousand to one hundred and seventy-five thousand off a brick of heroine. So Evil was hooked to the heroin money since day one. Corey liked the heroin money himself but preferred to sell crack or powder cocaine. Corey was considered the crack god in the streets because he would whip up thirty bricks and slang rock for rock. Selling crack gave Corey a rush and he loved being in the life of crack dealers. Corey was addicted to shaking and baking every day in the streets. He has a pack of young hyenas that he feeds. They love Corey and he loves them. Evil was flooding the streets with that fish scale when he got word through his people in Cincinnati that the Cincinnati Kats were planning an ambush on Evil and Corey. Evil got his people together and told them to be on high alert. Over the next few weeks, Evil and Corey ran under tight surveillance. Evil had gone to visit Wicked and had taken Wicked's mom also. Wicked's mom wanted to see her son because she hadn't been to see him in a while. Wicked knew that his mother was holding the family together.

Chapter 6:

The Ambush

Monique had just returned from Cincinnati, where she had gathered all the information that Evil and Corey needed to know. Monique's cousin, with whom she had grown up, had been living in Cincinnati for the past ten years. Ebony, Monique's cousin, is heavily involved with Big Sam. Big Sam is from Avondale in the Nati, and he has over one hundred soldiers. Evil met Big Sam years ago when he and Wicked had gone to the jazz festival in Cincinnati. Evil and Big Sam became business partners, and they moved a lot of weight up and down the highway. Word had gotten around that Evil was the only person that was still moving heavy weight on the cocaine level. Those Avondale boyz felt like since they had spent so much money with Evil, that Evil didn't respect their hustle or money. Corey and his boyz went to a club in Cincinnati chasing some of them natty hoes. While Corey and his boyz were in Cincinnati, they heard from one of them natty bitches that Corey and his crew better watch their backs. After investigating, Corey told Evil that Big Sam had planned to put a play down on them. Evil knew something had to be done about this. So Evil asked Monique, "Do you still fuck with your cousin Ebony?" Monique already heard about the play Big Sam was plotting and had told Evil that she was ten steps ahead of him. Evil asked Monique to get some of her thoroughbred bitches together and shoot to Cincinnati and find out exactly where them kat's be at. Within a couple of weeks, Monique discovered where them Kats eat, sleep, shit, and hustle. Now it was up to Evil to rock this Kat Big Sam all the way to sleep. Corey had the lil bitch he knew from Cincinnati holla at one of Big Sam's young boyz to see what they wanted to do with some of that fish scale? Shortly thereafter, the play was set for Big Sam and his boyz to buy seventy-five bricks of the fish scale. Big Sam had contacted Evil and set the play up for his people to meet Evil's people in Cleveland. They both agreed that Cleveland was a good spot because not too many people know about their business deals that went down in Cleveland. So, the night the deal was supposed to go down, Big Sam had already placed some of his people in Cleveland days ahead. What Big Sam didn't know

is that while they were fucking with Monique and her crew, these bitches

had already surrounded Big Sam's houses where the money and guns

were coming out of. Evil and Corey had everybody in position and when

it was time for them kat's in Cincinnati to move, as soon as they opened

their doors, dem boyz got walked right back into their houses. The

element of surprise took all of them boyz by storm. Each homie got shot

in the back of the head execution style, and the sign "Downtown" was

spray painted on the walls of all the houses where those dudes got

executed in. When Big Sam realized what had happened and knew that

his entire plan had gone down the drain, it was too late. He was stuck in

Cleveland and knew he was shark food. Monique called Evil and said,

"Babe that shit was too easy." Now these Avondale boyz beefing with

these Kats from downtown. Evil knew that they had pulled it off, and

then Cincinnati wouldn't or couldn't expect him to be a part of that

ambush on dem' clowns. Corey and his lil homies were ready to take

over shit everywhere. Evil told Corey to make sure that he keeps his boyz

in check, and not to have them running their mouths. Evil and Monique

sat back, and they both knew that more drama was certainly around the

corner. They knew that they had to be ready for it. Evil was feeling the pressure from everywhere. The police had turned up their heat. Kats in the streets were on one as well. Evil sat back and said to himself, "Damn I miss my nigga Wicked." He knew that despite having Corey and Monique, it wasn't the same as having his main Dogg by his side. Evil decided he had to take a much-needed vacation.

The television was blasting, and Corey sat in front of the TV as he watched his favorite movie Scarface. Nautica came into the room yelling, turn that shit down! Corey grabbed the remote and turned the TV up full blast, and quoted Scarface as he looked at Nautica and said in his Scarface voice "Say hello to my little friend." Nautica was annoyed at Corey, she threw her shoe at him, and said, "Turk on the phone." Corey grabbed the phone and said, "What's up homeboy?" Turk breathing heavily and said, "Man I found out where Jeff lives at." (Jeff is Big Sam's cousin). Now Turk had Corey's full attention. Turk explained to Corey how he was giving Alyson a ride home and saw Jeff. So, Turk said he had to be sure that it was Jeff before he spoke prematurely. He told Corey that Jeff lives with a white bitch in Washington Courthouse. Now shit was about to hit the fan. They waited for Jeff to come home. Corey found out that Jeff's bitch just had a baby. Corey knew this would be like taking candy from a baby. Jeff pulled into the parking lot in their space. When he exited the car, Jeff's girl reached behind her, and unhooked the baby seat that the newborn was in. Jeff went to the trunk of the car and grabbed a shopping bag. Corey and Turk watched as their homeboy laid on Jeff. As soon as Jeff put the key inside the keyhole, their young boys were all over his ass like back pockets. Corey and Turk watched his young homies grab Jeff's bitch and put the gun to her head. They could hear the bitch scream across the street from outside. The next thing they knew was that dem' boyz came running up out the spot with bags everywhere. The crew sat on the couch as they counted the money for the third time. This time Turk finally used the counting machine. After the third count, they came up with $2.3 million and some rare diamonds nobody knew anything about. What's so crazy is that everyone knew that Jeff and his family wouldn't be seen in Ohio anytime soon. Corey has been paying attention to the news lately, and what got his attention was every time he turned to the news, all he was hearing about was young Kat's killing shit. Turk had told Corey about that song Jeezy dropped on TM 103 called "Nothing." In that song, Turk was telling Corey how Jeezy was saying young people killing bout nothing.

Robyn called Corey and told him they were going to see Wicked in the morning. Told him that he should go. Corey was off papers, so he decided to go see his big brother from another mother. Wicked came out looking like he was making the time and time wasn't doing him. The last time Corey had seen Wicked was over four years ago. Since then, Wicked had put on at least 30 pounds of muscle. Wicked was glad to see Corey, and was also glad to see his old running friends. Selina was looking good and Robyn was looking good too. Wicked was pleased to have them back in his life. As the visit went on, Robyn told Wicked that she had found out who did that bullshit to Meagan's shop. Wicked not wanting to fuck his mood up told Robyn to let Corey and his homies handle that shit. Wicked has been hearing about Corey's boyz in the streets all over Ohio. Wicked told Corey that these young boyz are now crazy for real. Wicked emphasized to Corey to make sure he keeps those boyz busy, and not let them try to think for themselves or they will crash and burn! The visit was good, and they enjoyed each other's company. Wicked told his people that he would be home soon, and they all knew he was getting close. Corey took Wicked's advice and told Turk that they had to keep those young boyz busy. Corey found out who the kat was that smashed Meagan's shop, so he sent his homies to Nikki's strip club, which is out east off Mt. Vernon Ave. Corey told them to spray anything and everything in sight while the strip club was closing. Vic, who had broken into Meagan's shop, came out of the club with his entourage. Just as he opened the door to his Escalade, at least one hundred shots rang out right there on the spot and kat's were falling like bowling pins. By the time someone realized what happened, Corey's homies were on I-71 headed back north to Cleveland. The aftermath was crazy, the Columbus police called it the worst shooting in Columbus in the last twenty years. The whole city was buzzing about that incident, Corey and Turk were busy spreading the word that it was some CT boys that Vic and his homeboys had robbed. Everyone believed that story because "Vic was a scandalous nigga." Word on the street was Vic had stolen five bricks of work from his own brother. Nothing was the same anymore. Everywhere that Evil turned was somebody waiting in the shadows trying to tear his mouth out. Corey was experiencing the same thing from people on the streets. Everybody had been calling about the shit that went down in Cincinnati, and now that the feds had gotten involved, once big Sam got arrested for what the feds believed was some gang shit, it was really war in the streets. Before Evil and Monique could board the plane heading to Jamaica, they were processed for questioning in the shooting incident that went down on the west side of Columbus.

Chapter 7:

Family First

Wicked had the crowd rocking as he performed at the prison's talent show, it has been a while since he was on stage doing what he loved to do. It was his childhood friend Freeze that convinced Wicked to rock the mic for old time's sake. As usual, Wicked felt right at home on the stage as he did song after song. The inmates went crazy and Wicked knew that if all else failed once he gets home, he always had a career in the music game. Wicked knew that there were more important things going on in his life presently. He heard that Evil and Monique had been arrested. The news was shocking and Wicked was trying to figure out how exactly the shit went down. Wicked wasn't in contact with Evil as much as he used to be and Wicked was getting third-party information. The streets had been going through a major drought and Evil had been spending a lot of time ripping and running trying to get shit in order. Wicked and Evil didn't communicate that much, but once Wicked heard that Evil and Monique were arrested that quickly got his attention. So, he decided to contact Dan Orlosky to get the latest information about his right-hand man. Mr. Orlosky told Wicked that Evil and Monique's names came up in that Cincinnati shooting that left over twelve men dead. Wicked quickly knew from that information that Monique and Corey probably had more involvement than Evil did. Mr. Orlosky told Wicked that Monique had been released on one hundred-thousand-dollar bail. However, Mr. Orlosky told Wicked that the Attorney General requested no bail for Evil. Wicked asked, "how could the Attorney General get that off?" Mr. Orlosky assured Wicked that he knew a judge that could and would talk to him about getting Evil a bond. Mr. Orlosky told Wicked before he hung up that Evil would have to sit in jail for a few months. Wicked and his father Big Moose have developed a strong bond and have been working on strengthening their relationship. They have grown to care deeply for each other, and Big Moose is aware of the significance of spending quality time with his son while he still can. Both Wicked and Big Moose have been getting family visits together. In fact, the last visit that they had was somewhat of a family reunion. During the last visit, Wicked's mom and all his family were there. The very next day, Wicked was surprised by both Robyn and Selina who had been back in town for the past six months. These visits had given Wicked and his pops some much-needed family time. Wicked always remarked on how quickly time seemed to pass by during his visits with Mariah because he noticed that she was growing bigger and bigger every time he saw her. Mariah loved her dad, and enjoyed each moment they shared together. Mariah was so full of life that Wicked would be on the brink of tears after their visits together. The years Wicked lost from his daughter made him realize the importance of being a father and having a father in his life. Wicked knew that he has finally become a grown man.

Meagan knew that she has to help Wicked. She understood that with Evil being locked up and Corey running around like a chicken with his head cut off, someone had to step up. Meagan had talked to Monique on several separate occasions and learned what position Monique played. So, Meagan, being the mastermind herself, decided to pay Monique a personal visit in Cleveland. Ever since Meagan had been back in Wicked's life, the two of them made a pact with each other that nothing or nobody would ever come between them again. Meagan was still upset with herself for allowing the fact that she had missed Wicked so much drive her into another man's arm. From time-to-time, Meagan and Wicked would joke about her love affair with the country boy Antonio. However, Meagan quickly made it known to Wicked that Antonio might have been rich, but he was a bitch. Meagan arrived in Cleveland around 8 pm, and the heavy rain made driving difficult. Meagan hated driving in the rain. As she pulled into the horseshoe driveway, she noticed that Monique has a beautiful home to her surprise. Meagan has heard a lot about Monique but wasn't quite sure what to expect from this mystery woman. Monique greeted Meagan at the door and the two women shook hands and Monique escorted her in. The two women hit it off immediately. They talked and laughed like they had known each other for a million years. One thing the two prided themselves on was loyalty. Monique instantly took a liking to Meagan and could see why Wicked was in love with her. Hell, Monique was in love with Meagan. She thought long and hard about asking Meagan if she was into girls but quickly let that thought go out of respect for Wicked. Monique even told Meagan everything she needed to know about her relationship with Evil. Monique even told Meagan how she orchestrated the hits in Cincinnati. Meagan was impressed by Monique's ability to get that close to

Wicked's operation and to Evil's heart. Even though Meagan knew Evil had a soft dick when it came to females, it was so easy for Meagan to figure out how Monique was able to get close to Evil. She was baffled as to how Monique was able to convince Wicked to trust her. At any rate, Monique and Meagan became good friends. The two of them talked on the phone every day and made plans to run and create their own business. Evil had told Monique to manage the club Miracles for him while he awaited his fate. Monique asked Meagan to help her with the club. Meagan told Monique that they both knew enough people to open a couple of beauty salons and Monique immediately fell in love with the idea. Meagan told Wicked that she was going to open the beauty salon and have her mother and Wicked's mother run them. Wicked was cool with this idea of his mother running a beauty salon. He knew that Meagan was trying to make this an all-family affair and he loved it. Wicked called Meagan a mastermind, but it was Monique who really deserved all the credit for lighting that fire inside of her. Monique quickly discovered that once Meagan put her mind to something, nothing was going to stop her. Word spread throughout Columbus about this high-fashioned beauty salon. People from all over the city started to show up. One day out of the blue, Boo, who is Brittany's sister came strolling into the shop. Boo demanded to speak with Meagan and told Wicked's mother that she wanted Meagan to do her hair. Everybody in the shop knew Meagan didn't do hair but was the proprietor of the shop. Meagan got word that Boo wanted to see her, so she made her way to meet her. Meagan sat across from Boo and asked Boo why she was going around telling people that Wicked was still in love with her? Boo in return told Meagan that it was Wicked that was calling her phone at night and having her play with her pussy. Boo went on to say girl, if you're stupid enough to think Wicked is coming home to you then I guess you are dumber than you look! Boo knew that Meagan always hated her, so she felt like now was the time to rub the Facebook pictures she took with Wicked in Meagan's face. Unfortunately, Boo didn't know that Meagan already knew about the pictures. Meagan refused to give Boo the satisfaction of believing that she had succeeded in breaking her and Wicked up, despite seeing the pictures on Facebook. Everybody had found out that Meagan and Antonio had gotten together. It was all over the news because Antonio was this big-time athlete. Meagan was ten steps ahead of Boo and the game that she was playing. Meagan knew in her heart that Boo was going to be a potential problem.

Evil paced the floor constantly as he waited for Dan Orlosky to let him know what the judge said at his hearing about his bail. It seemed like hours had passed by when the C/O called Evil. When Evil looked at the clock, he realized that only twenty minutes had gone by. The C/O was seated at the table on the other end of the visiting room to give them some privacy. Mr. Orlosky already knew that the news he had for Evil would destroy him inside and out. Evil listened as Mr. Orlosky told him that the judge refused to set bail at any figure. Somehow some way the Attorney General had convinced the federal judge that Evil was a flight risk. Dan Orlosky told Evil that he was personally hiring some lawyers from D.C. to come to Columbus and aid him with this case. Evil has been charged with the R.I.C.O. and he has been implicated in two of the murders in Cincinnati. He was facing life in the federal prison system. Evil has a lot of support from people that were willing to do what they needed to do.

Wicked and his father had pulled all their resources together. Evil had over two thousand people fighting for his freedom. Monique was the ringleader; she was calling shots like the boss she knew she was. Monique had people as far as California involved with the movements, and the first thing Monique knew she had to do was start ending the people that were the problem. Monique had found out that Boo has been running her mouth to a lot of people about how she was going to be with

Wicked when he came home. Monique found this to be quite childish of

Boo, so Monique knew that Boo liked pussy just as much as she did.

Monique decided to invite Boo to dinner so the two of them could get to

know each other better. Just as Monique expected, Boo fell for the bait.

Monique was looking like a model on American's Next Top Model and

Boo was stunned. Boo thought she was in control of the situation from

the beginning to end, but she quickly saw how she allowed her emotions

to get the best of her. One thing Monique had over Boo and most females

like Boo, was that Monique didn't have a feeling in her big toe for

anything or anyone. People have no idea that Monique had been sexually

molested by her uncle and older men that would come around. She

understood how to play the game by the time she was twelve years old.

In fact, Monique was introduced to girls by her older cousin when she

was only eleven. So, Boo had no idea that she was fucking with the devil

in a Prada dress. Monique made Boo feel like she was the only person

on the planet, and for the next two weeks, Monique and Boo would meet

in ducked-off places. They would have the best sex little ol' Boo could

ever imagine. One day Monique asked Meagan if she could trust

Meagan, and Meagan responded by saying I've been trusting you this far. Monique already knew she could trust Meagan because she was Wicked's woman. Monique told Meagan that she was going to kill Boo because she was a live wire that had to go. Meagan looked at Monique and said, "Are you serious?" Monique said, "You'll know how serious I am when the time is right." Monique left Meagan at the beauty salon and Meagan thought to herself if Monique was being serious or not. It was breaking news, and the news reporter was on the TV saying how a woman was found dead inside the house. She died from smoke inhalation. The woman's name was released and sure enough, it was Bridgett Davis aka Boo. She was only 29 years old, and everybody felt bad for her except Monique. Meagan couldn't believe her eyes. Meagan was frozen in front of the TV shaking her head. She was startled by the phone ringing. She answered the phone and Monique was on the other end asking her if she had seen the news. Monique told Meagan that she needed to see her. Monique sat in the chair looking out the window of the club she had been running for Evil and said to Meagan, this is what must be done to people who pose a threat to us! Meagan sat and listened to Monique speak as if she was a trained assassin. Monique, knowing Meagan was feeling a little uneasy, told her not to worry. Meagan knew that she has a natural-born killer on her team and was feeling a sense of power. Both women knew what the other was thinking, and both said at the same time we must help Evil beat those charges. Evil has a major problem on his hands because of the two government witnesses that were going to testify against Evil and his involvement with Big Sam. These two could link Evil to Big Sam and to the killings in Cincinnati that day. Evil knew he had only one possibility as Dan Orlosky told him exactly what the two witnesses were going to testify to.

Wicked and Meagan talked about the events that had unfolded with the death of Boo. Meagan was telling Wicked how she felt about Monique being a certified Killa. Wicked had earlier learned that Monique was a gangster bitch from Evil bragging about her. So, he believed everything that Meagan was saying about her. Wicked was loving every moment of it. Mariah asked her daddy if she could have a puppy for her eighth birthday. Wicked couldn't believe that his little girl was turning eight years old the next week. Little Mariah knew she could get whatever she wanted from her father. She was a straight-A student. Meagan was extremely proud of Mariah and how she always performed well at school. Meagan was also a straight-A student when she was her daughter's age. Wicked knew the same couldn't be said about his academic accomplishments. Nevertheless, Wicked assured his daughter that she could and would have the puppy she wanted. Mariah loved Wicked so much and she cried every time she had to leave her father at the end of their visits. Meagan told Wicked that the beauty salon was doing well. Wicked was proud of Meagan and he knew that with just two years left, he had to start preparing his future with her and his daughter. Big Moose told Wicked that people from outside the prison would be coming in for a family day program. Big Moose told Wicked that this would be an opportunity to have Meagan come in and get some pussy. Wicked got so excited about the thought of getting some pussy that he almost busted a nut on the spot. The day the program was scheduled to take place, Meagan told Wicked that she had just started her period and that she wouldn't be off in time. So Wicked went into panic mode and decided to give Selina a call. Wicked explained the play to Selina and just like old times, Selina was down for the cause. The program started at approximately 8:30 am. Wicked watched Big Moose and his mother slip off in the back of the room. Wicked knew that his pops and mother were still in love after all these years. Selina wore a long black dress with no panties just like Wicked told her to do. Wicked and Selina made their way to the bathroom and the homie who was on the lookout said you have just ten minutes homies. Wicked didn't waste any time. Selina pulled her dress up over her back and Wicked stroked his dick until it was like a piece of metal. Selina knew she was about to get a good old fashion pounding but was cool with that. Wicked went straight to work and Selina felt every inch of Wicked's dick as he stretched her pussy with every stroke. Within minutes, Wicked had his dick in Selina's face watching her drink every drop of his nut. Wicked told Selina to put that pussy on his face because he wanted to suck it for old times' sake. Selina came to Wicked's face so fast they both had to laugh. Wicked and Selina knew their time was up as they made their way up out of the bathroom. Everyone was back seated together as if nothing had ever happened. Wicked found it hard to look at his mother knowing his pops just blew her back out, but Wicked knew they loved each other and wouldn't let any other person on planet earth get a shot of pussy, and he adored his mother for her commitment to his pops.

Tina was his angel, Mariah told Wicked at least a million times how much she loved her father. Wicked bought her the prettiest puppy she has ever seen. Mariah was so happy that her daddy loved her the way he did. Wicked told Meagan that he wanted her, his mom, and her mom to go on a cruise for a week and enjoy some time away. Wicked told Meagan that his sisters and Monique would look after the beauty salon so she wouldn't have to worry about them. After putting up a fight, Meagan agreed and so did the other two women in his life. Wicked was pleased with himself for sending the three women he adored so much on a cruise to enjoy some quality time. Selina and Robyn were back in Wicked's life now and Wicked thought to himself that he had to help Evil out and get Corey back on the right track and life would be good again. Wicked understood that family was the most important thing on this earth. Wicked told Big Moose as they worked out in the gym that family is first and everything else is second. Wicked knew his family was priority number one.

Chapter 8:

Young Nigga

Robyn told Wicked that she was on her way to pick Corey up from Belmont. Corey has been in Belmont Correctional for the past six months. He sat and waited for his sister to pull up in the parking lot. As Corey saw the silver BMW pull into the lot, he knew that he was a free man once again. Robyn parked the BMW and watched her little brother run towards the car. Robyn broke out laughing as Corey opened the car door and leaned over and kissed his big sister on the cheek. Robyn loved her brother but knew he was out of control. Robyn told Corey that Wicked was on the phone waiting to talk to him. Corey just did six months for driving on a suspended license and he had a nine-millimeter with hollow tip bullets. Dan Orlosky had gotten him the six months because the gun alone carried a mandatory five years. Corey knew Wicked was going to be on his ass about the importance of staying free. Corey used to think that Wicked had turned into this religious freak because he said all Wicked did nowadays was preach to everybody.

Just as Corey suspected, Wicked started blasting him on the phone about how fortunate he was to get only six months. Corey understood that Wicked had a genuine concern for him and Wicked had expressed to Corey at least a million times that he has mad love for him, and he only wanted the best for him. As the two men spoke on the phone, Robyn could see that whatever Wicked was saying to Corey really had his attention. Robyn asked Corey after he hung up with Wicked if he wanted something to eat. Corey told Robyn that his lil Redbone was waiting for him and he was going to eat her for breakfast, lunch, and dinner. Robyn knew things about Corey just weren't going to change, and his love for pussy surely wasn't one of them! Corey fucked his lil redbone like he had superhuman powers. Nautica looked at Corey and said damn my pussy is sore. Nautica told Corey he acts like he just did six years and not six months. Corey laughed at her, smacked her on the ass, and said now go fix me something to eat. The streets seemed so different for Corey. Wicked was still locked down. Evil was waiting for his trial to start, and some of his young Kats were locked up. For the first time in Corey's life, he knew that he had to make shit happen. Corey had learned a lot from Wicked when he was home, and he learned a lot from Evil too. Now Corey had to take what he learned from everybody and apply it to his life. He hit the streets immediately and started recruiting young dudes from everywhere, and his first stop was Cleveland. Corey got Monique and told her what his plans were, and Monique told him that these young boys in these streets nowadays don't play by any certain rules. She went on to school Corey and explain to him that all these young dudes care about is pussy, money, and respect. Corey knew Monique was right because what all the young Kats in Belmont talked about was pussy. Wicked had made sure Corey had a connection when he got out, and Evil left Corey a lot of his business. Corey knew that the only person that was going to stop Corey was Corey. Since he has done those six months, he understood how to network. Plus, he listened to them dudes in there and he knew the streets were still lightweight fucked up on the work side. Corey had in his possession, one hundred pounds of grand daddy, seven bricks of heroin, and twenty-two bricks of fish scale that Evil had left behind. Robyn called a meeting at her house. She had found a spot right outside of Akron, Ohio. Corey sat and listened as her dude from Chicago told Corey how to put it down in the streets. Charles was a top-notch hustler and Corey respected his opinion. The bottom line was he told Corey that in this game he had to get some young hungry dudes and show them that he loves them more than their mommas love them. Corey held on to every word, and when Charles was done talking to Corey, he was ready to take over Ohio. Corey hit the scene hard and linked up with Wicked's lil brother Reese who turned Corey on to some young Kats he knew from the 30th projects. These young dudes rode around with AKs and ARs like they were legal, but they were respected by everyone. Corey came through and showed them young fellas love on top of love. Corey would sell them shit so low that they thought Corey was sweet or a fool, but Corey was building his brand. He would take his young dudes out, and buy the bar out for his homies every time. Stunts like that drove these young dudes crazy. Corey would have Monique, Robyn, and Selina get some bitches together for his young dudes. He couldn't do any wrong in their eyes and to them Corey was God.

Corey had gone to his PO and ran into a homeboy that he knew from Belmont. The two exchanged numbers and Corey could tell from looking at him that he wasn't hitting for nothing. He remembered this Kat was an animal with his hands. Corey asked him where he was staying, and he said Cincinnati. He asked the young man if he was hustling, and he said yeah, I'm in the streets. His name is Steve and he told Corey he didn't know too much about Cincinnati because he was just getting his parole transferred there. Steve told Corey that he wasn't going to be in Columbus anymore, but he has a cousin that was out West doing his thing. Corey dapped him up and left. On his way home he called Monique and asked her if she still has contacts down in Cincinnati. Monique told Corey she has contacts everywhere. Later that day, Corey and a few of his young dudes were at the mall and ran into some young bitches from across town. These young bitches to Corey's surprise were about that life. He was still learning about Cleveland but knew that Columbus and Cleveland both had some gangster ass bitches. Corey and his lil homeboys hooked up with these bitches, and before they knew it, they had these young bitches sucking and fucking any and every one with a dick. Corey asked these bitches where they stay and one of the bitches said we are from E.C. That was short for East Cleveland. Corey had heard them E.C. boys eating, so Corey decided to take them E.C. boys up top. Monique, being a boss bitch herself, told Corey about the main guy from E.C. that was at her. She told Corey that he was buying anywhere from ten to fifteen bricks. Corey put the play in motion and had some of the young bitches he had recruited holla at them E.C. boys. They took the bait and were willing to meet, Corey wasn't a fool, so he had this pretty lil redbone, bowlegged bitch get at him with his pant down literally. Money Mike picked the lil redbone up and they went straight to the hotel. Within minutes, young killas kicked the front door open and snatched Money Mike up and put his bitch ass in the trunk of the car. Money Mike was so scared he pissed on himself before they pulled him out of the trunk. Once they had him tied up in the basement, Corey stabbed Money Mike in his legs and smashed his feet with a sledgehammer. Money Mike didn't know what to do. Corey told him to call and have five hundred thousand dropped off at a spot downtown. Money Mike kept swearing on his momma he didn't have five but could come up with three hundred thousand. Corey settled for the three but shot Money Mike in both of his eyes and cut his dick off and put it in his mouth. The only way the police or the coroner would be able to find Money Mike would be through dental records. The word traveled up and down. E.C. and the boys were shaken because Corey made sure that the rumor got out that some Cali boys were looking for Money Mike and his crew. Corey would tell them that he and his young gunners didn't bar any Cali boys or anybody. This move made Corey and his crew seem invincible. The streets of Cleveland weren't safe for anyone selling dope or hustling in the streets period. Corey and his homeboys had the whole city shaken and they were robbing everything that wasn't nailed down. The whole city was buying their work or heroin from Corey. He had his lil bitch Nautica so turned up she was pushing all the Kush in the city. It was a perfect look for Corey and now he felt like it was time for him to take his show on the road. Robyn and Corey were talking, and she was telling Corey about the Akron Kats and how much money they were getting. Robyn convinced Corey that Akron might be small, but the dudes were moving shit on a large scale. So, Corey took his sister's advice and visited Akron. Corey quickly saw that the Akron boys were more like New York niggas. This made shit even more compelling for Corey and his homeboys. Even the clubs in Akron seemed to be a bit wilder. The females were more down to party, and he loved that. Corey learned that the boys from the V were getting the most money. He had to meet them, so Robyn got in contact with some bitches she had met and introduced Corey and his boys to them. It was on and popping from that point on. Corey and his boys kicked it with these bitches for a few weeks learning as much as they could about the homies from the V.

Young Turk told Corey that they had to make a move fast if they were going to have the ups on these boys. Turk and Corey were best friends since they were kids. In fact, Turk is Nautica's brother. Corey has seen that look in Turk's eyes plenty of times to know that Turk was serious. Everybody got in position and headed to the apartment complex where the boys from the V. keep their money at. The plan was to lay on these dudes and when they pull up and put the key in the lock to open the door, surprise muthafucka. Corey and the crew waited for hours, and Corey started to think that Tracey might have changed her mind. Tracey was the set-up girl who found out where they keep their shit. She had started fucking a man named Ben who had the V on smash. It had just started to get dark when a money-green van pulled into the parking spot two cars away from Turk and Dave. Turk and Corey had at least ten young dudes with them ready to serve these boys. As Hen got out of the van, he yelled to one of his dudes to grab that shit out of Jimmy's trunk. Corey knew that they were about to hit them good, but before anybody could make a move Hen stood in front of the van and waited until an all-black Mustang pulled into the lot. Two dudes jumped out of the Mustang both carrying what looked like two duffle bags a piece. Corey and Turk both knew that they had just met during a drug transaction that was about to go down. Neither of them could believe their luck. Hen motioned to the two men from the mustang to follow him. That's when Corey and his crew made their move and crept up on them niggas like they were Navy Seals. Soon as he put the key in the door, they came out of nowhere from everywhere. Turk put the pistol grip Mossburg pump to the back of Hen's head and told him to open the muthafucking door. Corey had the two niggas from the Mustang scared with that SK with the beam on it in their faces, and the rest of the lil dudes had their men with them AKs on the rest of Hen's crew. Corey and Turk made sure all of them were inside the spot. Once everybody was in the spot, Corey went to work, he put on a show, speaking Jamaican and making Hen think that the man that was pistol-whipping him and his boys were the Jamaicans from Hilltop. After Corey and his young niggas got up out of there. Turk yelled over his shoulder your bitch ass better not come back to the Hilltop or you're dead! Corey laughed all the way back to Cleveland; everybody went to Miracles to drink and enjoy themselves. Corey was telling Monique what had gone down as Meagan walked in, Corey has not seen Meagan since she came back from the cruise. Meagan walked over to Corey and gave him a hug. Corey was happy to see Meagan and told her to tell Mariah that uncle Corey said hi. Corey gave Meagan five one-hundred-dollar bills and said that it was for Mariah. If Meagan kept half of the money she got for

Mariah, she would be a millionaire ten times over. Meagan was looking good as usual and told Monique that the beauty salon had gotten broken into while she was gone. Monique asked her if anything was stolen, and Meagan said no but whoever vandalized the place did it badly. Instantly Monique knew that it had to be some hating ass bitch that had one of their lame ass boyfriends do that. Meagan was in town visiting Wicked's sisters and stopped by Monique's house to tell her about the shop. Meagan knew Monique would have somebody investigate the situation. Meagan had become more focused on business trying to have shit in order by the time Wicked came home. Monique told Corey what had happened in Columbus and Corey knew that was going to be his next stop. Corey had been wanting to get back to Columbus so he could check out that shit he had been hearing about them niggas out West getting a lot of money. So once Corey and his homeboys hit Columbus, the hunt was on for Jeff. Steve told Corey that he was his cousin. Turk was originally from out West off Sullivan Ave., so he was familiar with most of the money getters, but Turk wasn't familiar with Jeff. He came to find out that Jeff is originally from Gary Indiana. Steve who told Corey about his fake ass cousin, forgot to mention that part. Corey and Turk understood that the GI boys weren't good in Columbus, so taking him up top was personal for Corey and Turk. It wasn't going to be an easy job, Jeff had protection like he was Obama. He didn't go anywhere by himself, and it was practically impossible to get something from him. Corey and Turk knew their backs were against the wall but he also knew Selina could help him out with this.

Dan Orlosky sat and rubbed his forehead as he discussed the legal ramification of Evil's legal situation. Dan Orlosky was convinced that his client was being implicated in these series of events based on his history with the criminal justice system. Ralph Demarco, one of the lawyers that Dan Orlosky had flown in from D.C., said that the government's entire case is circumstantial. The legal team that was assembled in this room is the best assembled since the O.J. Simpson trial. Everybody was calling Evil's legal team the Dream Team 2. The problem with this case is that there were so-called eyewitnesses who were willing to testify against Dan Orlosky's client. Evil couldn't believe that his fate relied on the testimony of some street thugs turned into government informants. Evil knew that the only way he would escape life in the federal system was to end these snitching muthafucka's that were lying against him. Evil had been in the county jail for four months now and the judge had put a no-contact order on him and Monique. He was missing Monique badly. Monique was communicating with Evil through people like Robyn, Selina, and Meagan. Evil knew that Corey had found someone that knew the person that was going to testify against him. On the last visit Evil had with Selina, she assured Evil that Corey and his young homies would be lying low in Cincinnati trying to find these lames. Evil told Selina to let Corey know that he was willing to pay one million dollars to him if he could find them. Meagan had come to visit Evil and had a message from Wicked. Meagan told Evil that Wicked and Big Moose were using their resources to help find them in Cincinnati. Evil understood that he has to be patient and prayed his friends and family came through for him. Evil was in the visiting room with his legal team when it hit him. Evil had been trying to convince Dan Orlosky to give him some information that could help him find out where the informants could be found. Dan Orlosky knew that Evil was desperate, and he knew that desperate people did desperate things. Dan Orlosky was at the top of his profession and wasn't willing to jeopardize his status because Evil was willing to pay him any amount of money for information that could get him thrown in federal prison himself. So as Evil sat with his legal team it hit him. Evil knew that his best shot at getting the information he wanted was to convince Dan Orlosky's personal secretary to help him. Alyson Swank has been working at the Orlosky law firm for the past three years. She is pretty with long red hair. She has the type of beauty that made an average man smile when she walked in the room. But what Alyson really has that separated her from most red-haired white girls was that all she has ever been involved with were big dick black men. Most of the men at Orlosky's law firm were the typical white guys with their law degrees and drank Coors Light. Frankly, those types of men were a complete turn off for Alyson. Monique has been watching Alyson and has finally felt it was time for her to make a move. Alyson sipped her favorite drink and began to read the legal news when Monique approached her. Alyson not knowing who this beautiful black woman standing before her was asked, "may I help you?" Monique responded, "yes, you can help me."

It didn't take Monique long to realize Alyson wasn't your typical red-haired perky white girl. Monique had Alyson laughing and telling her that it was the swag she had for a white girl that drew Monique's attention. Monique had learned from their conversation that Alyson was crazy about black men. The two women talked and hung out every day for the next few weeks. One day Monique told Alyson that she has somebody that she might be interested in. Alyson having a weakness for a black man with swag was blown off her feet when she saw Turk. Monique already told Turk everything he needed to know about Alyson. Monique reminded Turk of the importance of getting Alyson to give us the paperwork needed to help Evil. The date was going well, and Alyson was really feeling Turk. They made their way to the dance floor and Turk had Alyson's panties soaked and wet. Before the place was closing Alyson whispered in Turk's ear, you ready to go? Turk had Alyson's arms wrapped around his neck as he held her in the air. Alyson has never had anyone fuck her like this and Turk had taken two pills and sipped some lean. Alyson's pussy was so wet that Turk asked her if she pissed on him? Turk fucked Alyson all night and she came like never before. Alyson called Turk every day and they kicked it hard. Turk finally convinced Alyson to spy on Dan Orlosky and see if she could catch him slipping to sneak a peek at his files.

Chapter 9:

Politics As Usual

Alyson couldn't believe her eyes as she stared at the computer screen. Alyson had come to Mr. Orlosky's office to retrieve the paperwork for the upcoming trial. However, Alyson saw this as an opportunity to see if she could find anything to help Evil. What Alyson was looking at made her skin crawl. She knew Mr. Orlosky was in a meeting so she knew she had to go around his office. She looked around and noticed a light blinking on Mr. Orlosky's computer. Mr. Orlosky had forgotten to close out the window on his computer screen. Alyson pressed enter on the computer and over a thousand images of kiddy porn appeared on the screen. Alyson knew she had to move fast so she sent these images to Monique's phone. Monique told Alyson she had done well and should get out of the office before she got caught. Dan Orlosky is well respected in Reynoldsburg, Ohio in the suburbs outside of Columbus. He is also a member of the school board committee. Mrs. Orlosky is the Director of Athletics for the high school. Mrs. Orlosky also helps with local charities such as Red Cross and Goodwill. The Orlosky's have two children, both in college. They have been married for over twenty-five years and have three grandchildren. Dan Orlosky knew that his sickness would be his downfall. Mr. Orlosky kept telling himself that he would find a way to get help. But he was trapped in a world he couldn't afford to let anyone find out. Dan Orlosky got a phone call from Monique who demanded to meet with him. He immediately knew this was a strange call because he has nothing to discuss with Monique. He told Monique that there were many scheduled appointments he has to attend. Monique, knowing she was getting the spin move, told Mr. Orlosky that it was imperative that he met her at once. He couldn't understand that his life was in the palm of this gun toting drug dealer's bitch. Monique knew she had Dan Orlosky's attention and went to work. Monique cutting straight to the chase told Dan Orlosky that she needs the whereabouts of the two government witnesses or she would go to 10 TV News with her pictures of Dan Orlosky and his love for little boys. Dan Orlosky knew he had no win. He pleaded with Monique to give him a few weeks to make a few moves to come up with something she could use. Dan Orlosky knew that his life was totally in Monique's hands, and he felt like he was going to throw up. Monique understood that Dan Orlosky was worried out of his mind that she would ruin him, so she assured him that he has nothing to worry about. Monique stood and told Dan Orlosky he has exactly three weeks to have that information or say goodbye to his wife and career. Turk gave Alyson fifty thousand dollars for getting those pictures. Alyson thought to herself that she would even have those pictures for free. All Alyson cared about was Turk and that good dick she was getting. Megan and Monique agreed that Wicked should know about the information they had on Dan Orlosky. Meagan watched Wicked as he damn nearly fainted after hearing about Dan Orlosky. Wicked was so proud of Monique and everybody who played a role. All Wicked kept saying to Meagan was Evil was going to walk and his best friend would be home for his release. Wicked played with his daughter for the rest of the visit. Meagan felt good knowing her man was happy. Wicked told pops about the news, and Big Moose knew politics well. Big Moose told Wicked that Dan Orlosky wasn't going to go out silently so be ready for anything. Big Moose told Wicked they call this game "Political Science

101." Corey and Turk carefully rode through the streets of Cincinnati trying to find Steve that Corey knew. Steve is hard to find, and no one knows who he is. Corey remembered when they were locked up together that he mentioned his sister lived in Cincinnati. Corey put the word out to find Steve's sister. Her name is Kesha, and she ran a daycare center. Within a few days, Corey was face to face with the girl of his dreams. Kesha is so fine that Corey was stuck and couldn't go past her. Kesha told Corey that Steve was in jail for robbing the gas station a month ago. Corey couldn't understand why Steve was a loser like that. Kesha has a man that is heavy in the heroin game. Black heard about Corey sweating his girl and going to the daycare center every day. Kesha told Corey that her man Black was upset that he was coming to the daycare center every day. Corey not thinking to let his ego get in his way told Kesha that he would take her from Black. But what Corey didn't realize was Kesha was a loyal ass Bitch to her man. Kesha and Black were childhood lovers and had already been battle tested. Kesha knew Corey had to go; Black isn't a fool by far. He had shit on smash and is a street gangster to the core. Corey was playing a dangerous game and was allowing his lust and ego to cloud his better judgment. Turk knew something was bothering Corey because Corey always seemed distracted. Corey, knowing he shouldn't go to the daycare center decided to go anyway. Kesha shook her head as Corey walked in. She had just talked to Black, and Black had made a run to the west side, but he would be back. Corey had no idea that Black was going to be pulling up while he was there meeting with his girl. Turk had asked Corey where he was about to go but Corey lied to Turk. Corey told Turk he was just going to make a run to McDonald's so Turk told Corey to bring him a spicy chicken combo meal. Black has done his homework on Corey and he knew Corey was from Columbus and he is a young gunner. Black has some young gunners himself and he knew that Corey was on some bullshit. To Black, Corey was just another thug in the streets that was after his money and girl. As Corey tried to make his move on Kesha, he saw a black-on-black Maybach pull up. Black and two of his goons jumped out of the car. Corey knew this encounter was about to get ugly. At that moment Corey realized he didn't have his vest on, Black entered the daycare and Kesha knowing her man met him at the door. Black pushed Kesha to the side and confronted Corey. Black called Corey a bitch ass nigga and told Corey to come outside away from the kids. Once again Corey allowed his ego to get in the way of his better judgment. Corey ran outside towards Black thinking he was going to kill his hoe ass for calling him a bitch. Corey pulled his nine out and asked Black, "what the fuck did you call me?" Black threw his hands in the air and said it's your world playa. Corey never saw the shots fired, as he felt the burning sensation running down his legs. Corey was turned around by the bullet that hit him in the arm the second time. As Corey did a 360, he let off as many shots as he could. By now Corey's adrenaline was racing and he knew he had to shoot his way out or die on the spot. Police sirens could be heard as Black and his boys sped off. Corey stumbled to his Tahoe and barely was able to open the door. Man, Turk couldn't believe Corey had been shot. They rushed Corey to a hospital in Hamilton, Ohio not wanting the local police to arrest him on sight. The doctors at the ER said Corey had been shot three times and was extremely lucky to be alive. All three bullets went through and through just missing major arteries. Corey was shot in the forearm, leg, and shoulder. Turk was being bombarded with questions about what had happened. He was angry with Corey because he knew what Corey had told him earlier. Meanwhile, Robyn received news that Corey had been shot, but thankfully, he would survive. Although she loved her little brother, she was aware of his tendency to behave recklessly. Nautica was going crazy trying to figure out what happened. She was furious with Turk and couldn't believe he left Corey's side. It seemed as if nobody believed that Turk didn't know how or what really went down. All Turk knew he was going to find out what happened... Corey stayed in the hospital for a week and after he was released from the hospital, Turk had listened to Monique, and everybody went back to Columbus. They have been staying at a hotel downtown in Cincinnati. Once Corey was feeling better, everyone wanted to know what happened and who shot Corey. The only person who knew about Kesha was Turk, but Turk wasn't about to mention Kesha in front of Nautica. The word got out that Corey was set up and some Kats tried to rob him. That was the story that Corey put out there. Corey knew that he had allowed his lust for women to almost cost him his life. Monique told Corey to just chill out and heal all the way up. Monique got the call she had been waiting for. Dan Orlosky texted her the address to meet him. He was a private man and made Monique give her word that she would be by herself during this meeting. Monique wasn't familiar with Dublin, Ohio but Dan Orlosky has a house there and that's where he wanted to meet. Monique went through every piece of paperwork like she was a detective after examining everything Monique knew she has what she needed. The two shook hands and Dan Orlosky told Monique that his life was on the line. Monique assured Dan Orlosky that it wasn't him she was after. She assembled her team and made everyone to understand that the stakes were extremely high, and failure wasn't a choice in this! They learned that the two government witnesses were being held at Hotel 6 in Jackson, Ohio. Both women knew that the best witness was a dead witness.

Both Meagan and Monique knew that it was in their hands to get this job done. Meagan has a friend that got all the staff liaison at Hotel 6. Now it was a matter of looking into their backgrounds to see which one could be bought. The Hotel staff was small, so this made everybody's job easier than expected. Robyn learned that the Marshalls changed shifts three times a day. So, the crew figured that whenever they made their move, it would have to be done during shift change. Meagan was explaining to everyone, especially the young boys that this whole operation would be done on her call and her command. She went on to explain to the young boys that their role in this would be huge, so they really had to be on point. Evil was a nervous wreck when Meagan, Selina, and Robyn all went to visit him. As Meagan explained to Evil to relax and trust their plan, Evil kept reminding them that he was facing life. Evil didn't need to remind them because it was Meagan and company that kept reminding themselves that Evil was facing life. Besides, Wicked and Big Moose knew Evil's situation. Nevertheless, the visit did Evil some good because his trial was only four weeks away. Meagan didn't mention anything to Evil. The women embraced Evil and each of them hugged their friend tightly while expressing their love and support, assuring him that everything would be alright. Selina met with Rose and the two women went over Rose's daily activities. Rose has been working for Hotel 6 for the past two years. She is an older Hispanic woman that worked hard. All members of the hotel management loved Rose and her work ethic. However, what the hotel management didn't know was that Rose always felt underpaid. She has been waiting for a raise for the past six months to enable her to buy a car for her daughter and granddaughter. Selina has been watching Rose closely and saw that she needed help financially. Rose finally agreed to meet with Selina and the two of them talked. Selina convinced Rose that the management at Hotel 6 didn't appreciate her. Selina made Rose believe that if she helped her gain access to the hotel, she would give her twenty thousand dollars cash. Rose knew that if she got twenty thousand dollars in her possession, her life would never be the same. After a few more meetings, she accepted and received a ten-thousand-dollar advance payment. Selina had full access to the Hotel. Monique sat at the table as the other women sat around the table like a scene from the movie, "Godfather." Monique looked around the table and explained to every woman at the table exactly what their individual jobs were. The day the move was to take place, all the women that were going to be inside the Hotel would be wearing the Hotel 6 uniforms. These women would be dressed as housekeepers and cleaners. Monique has women that would be working the front desk and working certain floors. Meagan, Selina, and Robyn would coordinate the ground attack from outside. As the women prepared to narrow down the specific day to execute their plan, the two men that were going to testify had been spotted. They were living on the third floor and went to the gym every morning at approximately 6:00 am. Now Monique knew that every morning at 5:45 am the morning shift would change, and she knew that the women inside had exactly six minutes to get inside the gym and be waiting for them. Over the next couple of days, the women placed themselves in different positions throughout the hotel. The only thing left to do now Monique said is to make sure these young gunners are on point! The day finally arrived, and it was pouring. Monique and Meagan along with Selina and Robyn had been at the adjacent building since the day before. They were all in the right places and the women communicated via an earpiece that the Hotel 6 staff were already using. As the time got closer and closer, their adrenaline was pumping like crazy. At approximately 5:48 am the three hired women slipped into the gym. Each woman had carefully installed a silencer on their gun. The three women had on all black and were ready to execute the play. As they waited, Monique quickly asked Sheila, "Is everything good?" Sheila told Monique that everything was great. At that moment two cars pulled into the Hotel 6 parking lot. Each car has four people in it. Within minutes both carloads of people were standing in the parking lot. The men were arguing about some money that was missing. The next thing you know gunshots rang out just as the feds were changing shifts. As this big commotion went on outside, the two men were being escorted to the gym. Once the feds had them safely in the gym, they locked the gym doors and told them to stay put. The two never saw the women as they appeared out of nowhere. Shelia placed each shot in the middle of their foreheads at close blank range. Both of their throats were cut with a scalpel from ear to ear. The three women made their way out of the hotel by using the back exit. As the feds and local police tried to defuse the scene, Monique and the gang made their way out of the adjacent building. Once the feds had complete control of the parking lot scene, they took all eight men into custody without injury. The two federal US Marshals that had just come on shift went to the gym to sit with the two government informants. However, neither one of the Marshals was expecting to walk into the horrific scene that was in front of them. Both two government witnesses were lying directly on their backs with their eyes wide open. As the Marshals got up to see the two dead bodies in front of them, they discovered that the men had been shot in the forehead at close range and their throats sliced. The Marshals drew their weapons as they called for backup and had the building locked down. The feds searched the hotel up and down but came up with nothing. They interviewed every staff member that was on shift at least a million times. In every angle that the feds searched, they came up empty. The eight men that Monique and Meagan had hired all stuck to their story. The eight men told the feds that they were from out of town. Their story was simple, they didn't know anybody, so they were going to get a room and wait to meet the other guys that pulled up. All the feds got from these dudes was somebody in their crew got shorted some money and they wanted their money. All the men involved in the shooting were being held until further notice. It was breaking news, Monique, and Meagan knew they had pulled it off. Meagan was saying to Robyn, them bitches "Set It Off." They don't have shit on us. Everybody was happy. The headlines were saying that the government witnesses were gunned down in cold blood. Now the rumor was buzzing that Evil had so much power he had those two executed. Dan Orlosky couldn't believe his luck. He knew without any doubt that the Attorney General's office's whole case was surrounded by the dead witnesses' testimony. Without their testimony, Dan Orlosky knew Evil would walk. Evil asked Dan Orlosky repeatedly, "are you sure they can't bring up anything else?" Dan Orlosky understood Evil's concern but assured him that the most he could be facing now is minor drug charges. Dan Orlosky understood that pursuing a minor drug charge against Evil was unlikely since the government had built their case around Racketeering and Murder charges. As per legal knowledge, a case without a witness is usually difficult to win. Evil wanted to know what was next about his freedom. Dan Orlosky told him that he would go to the Attorney General and ask him what he is planning to do with the case now. Dan Orlosky told Evil he should have him free within the next few weeks. Evil felt like a new man, smiled to himself, and said damn what would I do without you Wicked? The feds were turning everything upside down but weren't getting anywhere. The CIA had been brought in to investigate the agents that handled the incident that took place. It seemed like an inside job and the FBI was in turmoil.

Evil looked at Monique and said damn babe look how clear this water is, Evil sipped on his tropical drink as he enjoyed the breeze from the Pacific Ocean. Monique has always wanted to go to Bora Bora and now she was here living the life she always dreamed of. The whole gang had come along to celebrate Evil's second chance at life. Meagan, Selina, Robyn, Corey, Turk, Nautica, and Alyson were all there. Evil still couldn't believe that his family had pulled off the unthinkable. All Evil kept saying to Monique was "did you see the Attorney General's face as the judge had to dismiss the case?" Evil reflected on his situation and reminded himself of what he had just been through. All Evil kept saying over and over was those words the judge said in court. Will the defendant please stand.... The judge went on to say it has been brought to the court's attention that the Government is dropping all charges against Mr. Deon Smith. Evil couldn't do anything but smile as he looked at his babe Monique and contemplated how this bitch learned to be so gangster. Evil knew he was glad she was on his side and not the other side. Ever since Evil got released and the media put all that shit out there about Evil going to war against the government and winning, he has been declared the new crime boss of Ohio. This newfound fame and celebrity status enabled Evil to get VIP treatment everywhere he went. It seemed like the entire world knew who he was, and Evil, not letting this opportunity get away, took full advantage of it. Monique knew that Evil was on cloud nine; she also knew that Evil had all the money, power, and respect. This was a dangerous combination, but Monique knew she had to keep him grounded. Evil traveled all over the world. He sent Wicked pictures from Hawaii while swimming with the sharks, and even pictures from as far as Morocco. Evil had built an empire that was steadily rising. Nothing or nobody could stop him.

Wicked was happy for Evil and his newfound success. He knew that Evil has a new outlook on life, but what Wicked really knew was that Evil was unaware of his actual involvement in everything that took place with Evil. Wicked always knew that no matter how much money Evil got or how many bitches Evil had, Wicked would always have to protect him from the wolves. Robyn made a comment to Evil one day and Evil said he would never forget what she said. Robyn told Evil a long time ago that he wasn't shit without Wicked. Now as Evil sat in a condominium overlooking downtown Miami, he thought to himself, yes Robyn, I thought I wasn't going to be shit without Wicked. Evil, being the type to never forget shit sat back and remembered everything anybody has ever done or said to him. All Evil knew was that he was going to show the world that he could make it without Wicked holding his hand. Evil was doing good for himself and had opened a chain of upscale nightclubs in Miami. He also established a chain of classy seafood restaurants in Miami. He made Miami his home and Monique was right by his side. Monique convinced Evil to open some stuff in Houston where he had family on his father's side. Evil followed Monique's advice and bought over twenty houses and stores in Houston within months. Back in Ohio, Evil decided to open a strip club in Columbus called WICKEDS. Evil knew that Wicked would love the fact that his homeboy got him his own club in his name. Evil has always envisioned himself and Wicked's names in bright lights. Now all he wanted to do is to impress Wicked and let his bro know that his boy held it down for the whole ten years that Wicked was gone. Evil found himself from time to time reminiscing about how he and Wicked came up together from day one. Evil really missed Wicked. He wanted the entire world to know that Wicked was coming home soon.

The FBI was in full attack mode, and they had turned their investigation up on Evil and any member of his crew. Every hustler in the streets was feeling the effects of Evil beating his case against the government. Kats were getting pulled over for nothing. The police in every city were clowning and shooting. The world had seemed like it changed since Evil beat the charges like Rocky. Young boyz have been getting it bad and there were at least ten shootings that involved a young man getting shot by the police for wearing hoodies. Evil has been paying attention to the latest events that were happening around the country. Corey was damn near back to his old self health-wise. He wasn't 100 percent just yet, but Corey wasn't limping as much as he used to. He has been relatively quiet since the shooting in Cincinnati. All Corey had in his mind was killing Black and the two people he was with. He has been investigating Black ever since he got out of the hospital. Corey learned that Black has done five years for felonious assault for shooting a narc. He knew Black was a street thug, but Corey wasn't going to rest until he got his man. Evil and Corey have been hanging out lately. The two of them were playing Madden at one of Evil's houses in Cleveland. Evil saw this as an opportunity to kick it with his lil bro. Evil asked Corey what had happened when he got shot. Evil saw that Corey didn't really want to speak about the incident, so he didn't push it but knew he had to find out. Evil did tell Corey that whoever is your enemy is my enemy. Corey knew where Evil was coming from. Dan Orlosky had contacted Monique and requested to meet with her privately. Dan Orlosky hasn't seen Monique since their last meeting. He wanted to thank Monique for saving his career and marriage. Monique reminded him that it wasn't you that I was after. She asked Dan Orlosky, "what's the deal with the guys that got arrested for shooting in the parking lot back then?" He told Monique that most of them were being charged with federal possession of a firearm and had been charged with a gang specification. Dan Orlosky told Monique, the bottom line is that the guys would be facing anywhere from ten to twenty years in the feds. Monique thought to herself that no matter how much they paid them it was worth every penny. After the case against Evil, Dan Orlosky's law firm has been getting plenty of business. He was considered the modern-day Johnny Cochran.

Evil spent most of his time with Miracle and Mariah. He loved spending time with his two favorite girls. Wicked's daughter Mariah loved her godfather. Ever since Evil won his case against the government, he would buy Mariah whatever he bought Miracle. He took Mariah and Miracle to visit Wicked every Sunday; in fact, Evil took Tina along with them every Sunday. Wicked was thankful to have Evil back on the stage. He knew Evil would look after his mother and make sure she was straight. Evil always loved and cared for Tina because she has been more of a mother to him than his own mother. Even after Evil's mother passed,

Tina made sure Evil was good. She often cooked Evil his favorite foods and helped with Miracle. She even made sure Evil's mother's funeral arrangements were right. Evil knew that without Tina being there for him, he didn't know what he would have done. Evil and Wicked discussed everything under the sun, and they knew that once Wicked got out, everybody would be watching their every move. Evil told Wicked on a visit that he appreciated Wicked because he has always been there for him. He told Wicked that getting his business degree allowed him to get a certain property that the bank wouldn't give the ordinary Joe. Wicked knew that having that business degree would come in handy. Evil was sharp and was coming into his own. He started to build an empire and a new army of soldiers. Evil has home boys from everywhere that he could call. It was nothing for Evil to make a phone call in Houston even if he was in Miami. Evil learned from Wicked that fear preserves order and now he was loved by few, hated by many but respected by all. He finally knew the feeling of having muthafuckas at your beck and call. Evil watched Scarface as he sat in his hot tub and said to himself, "Evil, the world is yours."

Wicked and Black talked on the phone and Black was explaining to him the shit he had just gone through. Black and Wicked have become close and the two of them were like brothers. Black had done five years for shooting some kat who was playing with his money. Wicked met Black when he first arrived in Lancaster. The two hit it off right out the gate. They had the same goals and visions. It was Black that encouraged Wicked to pursue his business degree. Black is involved with the music industry and told Wicked to focus his mind on the music game as well. Wicked has been spending a lot of time trying to learn how to start his own record label and become a multi-talented producer. Wicked knew since his early days of running in the streets that thugs from all levels of society love bitches and pussy. Wicked understood that if he could own his business, he would have the baddest bitches connected to his name and record label. Black told Wicked about Corey from Columbus that was sweating Kesha. He also told Wicked how Corey was being very disrespectful. Wicked had a strong feeling that Black was talking about his Corey. Wicked asked Black, "Was this Corey you're talking about shot in Cincinnati?" Black responded, "yes how did you know that?" Wicked took a deep breath then finally spoke into the phone and said, "damn my nigga, that's my young nigga." Black was silent, knowing that this whole situation just got worse. Black broke his silence and asked Wicked what he should do. Wicked didn't know much about what happened because Corey has been keeping a tight lid on the shit. So Wicked told Black that he would talk to Corey and see what he could find out. Black told Wicked that he appreciated that and that he would send Wicked some more pictures. Corey was angry and didn't want Wicked to try to squash the beef between him and Black. Every time Corey looked in the mirror and saw those bullet wounds, he knew he was going to kill Black.

Evil was going over the damage from the hurricane that hit Miami. He knew that it was always a possibility that a hurricane or flood could destroy one of his properties. Miami has too much to offer so Evil couldn't resist living next to South Beach. Monique has taken to Miami and all its beautiful women quite well. She has been mistaken for Gabriel Union at least ten times. Although Monique knew she was a sexy and beautiful woman, she knew that Evil couldn't resist the temptation on the island. Miami has so many different sexy women from all over the world. She has kept a few secrets from Evil and the fact that she likes pussy was one of them. Evil's birthday was coming up in less than a week so Monique decided to give him a birthday present he would never forget. One night, Evil and Monique went to one of their favorite night clubs and Monique saw this Latin woman with a body out of this world.

She asked Evil, "did you find this woman attractive?" Evil being a sucka for bad bitches smiled at Monique and said "yes, she's cool." As the night went on, Monique told Evil that she wants to go for a run, and would meet him back at the condominium later. Evil was at that condominium chilling when Monique came home but what Evil didn't know was that Monique brought that bad Latin bitch home with her. When Monique walked into the bedroom with that Latin bitch, Evil couldn't believe his eyes. Monique looked at Evil and said, "Happy Birthday babe." Monique undressed the Latin bitch while Evil watched. He was so shocked at how Monique and that Latin bitch acted like he wasn't even in the room. The women sucked each other's pussy like nothing he has seen before and when Monique made the Latin bitch cum, Monique told the Latin bitch to squirt on her face. Monique called Evil to join them. He had gotten butt ass naked with his dick already hard. Monique and the Latin bitch took turns licking Evil's dick until he couldn't take it anymore. Monique asked the Latin bitch to climb up on Evil's dick while he lay on his back. Monique sat on Evil's face so he could taste that wet sweet pussy of hers. He knew he had hit a lick with Monique. As Evil came, Monique and the Latin bitch allowed him to paint their faces with his cum. Monique looked at Evil as he lay on the bed and said Happy Birthday daddy.

Wicked knew he had a fucked-up situation on his hands. He knew Corey was a hothead, and also knew Black would kill Corey in a minute. So, his mind was racing, and he knew something had to give. Wicked was telling Robyn about the situation and Robyn told Wicked to talk to Nautica. Wicked really didn't know Nautica but knew he had to talk to her. Nautica was cool and she understood where Wicked was coming from plus Nautica was in love with Corey and didn't want Corey to go back to jail or the graveyard. They both agreed that they have to keep trying to talk some sense into Corey. Wicked even had Turk talk to Corey, and although he knew that everyone was giving him the right advice, Corey wasn't willing to listen.

Chapter 10:

Penitentiary Chances

Wicked thought to himself; 2 Pac said it best, "penitentiaries is packed with promise makers." It has been damn near nine years since Wicked has been locked up, but what he couldn't understand was how in the fuck people could come back and forth to the joint. He has seen homies leave the joint and within ninety days they would be back. The shit was unbelievable how they sat around and told all these lies about what they were going to do once they got back out. Wicked has seen it time after time. These same people went home and either got killed or they were right back asking for a care package. To some of them, Wicked thought he had it better in the joint than they did on the streets. It was amazing how they would sit around and tell all these fake ass stories. He used to think when he first got locked up that wannabe in the joint was too gangster for TV. Now he understood that a person could be all he wanted to be in the joint, but Wicked did meet some real thugs in the joint. One thing you could count on was no matter what, you were going to meet people from every city in Ohio with a different story and that's exactly what Wicked did. He met Kats from all over Ohio and found out that each one from each city acted a certain type of way. For example, Wicked never really got along with Cleveland boyz when he first got locked up. To Wicked, Cleveland boyz thought they were the roughest, and toughest, guys on earth. He felt like Akron Kats thought they had a New York type of swag. Even the ones from the smaller cities up north felt like they were the shit and muthafucka's had to recognize them. Wicked got along with the Dayton thugs very well. To Wicked, these Dayton thugs were all about getting money and that's all he was into. Wicked used to trip on his Columbus homies and he would always say to them Columbus Kats, "Why the fuck does everything have to be about who's hood the toughest?" Wicked couldn't understand that Columbus Kats acted like Cali boys. Columbus was the murder capital in Ohio, and Wicked didn't want any part of that shit. He felt like Columbus boys cost him ten years of his young life, but it was the Cincinnati Kats that amused

Wicked the most. They had a completely different vibe and swag than the rest of the Ohio boys. These Cincinnati Kats rocked gold teeth heavily like down south. Wicked knew the Cincinnati Kats talked with a down south slang. Everything about Cincinnati Kats represented something about the south. Wicked learned over the years that every city in Ohio has its good and bad, but what Wicked wanted to do was build something strong with all the real ones from each city and make money. As time went by, the penitentiary taught Wicked all sorts of life skills. He learned that it wasn't that much of a difference in the joint from the streets. Everyone in the joint was getting money, pussy, and respect. The penitentiary made Wicked even more dangerous. This time that Wicked has done allowed him the opportunity to find himself. He has taken full advantage of everything that prison had to offer. When Wicked first got locked up, he used to wonder why people went to church and attended jail programs like NA and AA. However, as time went by, Wicked began to see the shit that was going on behind the scenes. He wasn't a fool. Wicked started to figure out that if you wanted to meet people from the outside, you had to go where they were at. Wicked used to listen to homies tell him all the time about the thirsty ass bitches that be coming in from the streets. He started to attend all the different programs and realized what he has been missing. Wicked's Homeboy, Black from Cincinnati has a bitch that worked for some agency that use to come to the prison and give motivational speeches, but Black was to grab his pack from one of the women that came in. Wicked was impressed at how the shit went down and had to be a part of it. He was on a mission and knew that if he was locked up, he would make each day a better day. Meagan was supportive of anything that he was trying to put down. She believed in her man and knew that he would make something out of nothing. Meagan has been coming to see Wicked every Saturday now for the past year and a half. This was their time because Meagan brought Mariah to see her daddy on Sundays. Evil would come sometimes but would also let Meagan have her time. Prison made the Wicked family come together and become one solid foundation. Wicked would constantly tell Meagan that this time had made him a better man, and Meagan could see the shine in Wicked. She was proud of Wicked because he kept his focus on the big picture of coming home. Wicked's mother would split her visits in half so she could spend time with Wicked and his pops. Wicked would go back to his dorm after every visit and meditate on all the things that had happened in his life over the years. One thing Wicked knew was he was on his way home and he was going to be the next Bill Gates. Wicked had met this lil female named TT. He met her through his homeboy from out south in Columbus. TT was getting money in Atlanta and Miami fucking with the porn industry. Wicked knew that if he could link up with TT, she could build his female fan base up with his music. Wicked and TT have a lot in common and TT was down with the program. Now all Wicked had to do was create his record label and make TT the face on the female side of it. Wicked knew he has come a long way, but he also knew he has a long way to go. He knew that no matter what, he had to take advantage of anything and everything the penitentiary has to offer. Evil kept telling Wicked about all the local rap artists in Ohio that were willing to talk. Wicked has plans to unite all Ohio rappers and put them under his label. This has been his plan for a while now. Wicked thought he was the next Jay Z.

Corey knew his options were slim to none. The only thing Corey kept thinking about was killing Black. Corey wasn't feeling Wicked; he knew now that Black and Wicked were friends while Black was locked up with Wicked. That shit didn't mean anything to Corey. The odds were stacked against young Corey. The only person Corey thought would ride with him on Black was Turk, but Corey knew that Turk had mad respect for Wicked. There were so many young boys getting swooped up by the new gang task force in Columbus. The streets were on fire because the feds were still turning up the heat from Evil winning the case against the government. Corey was fully aware that going to war with Black was a recipe for disaster. Turk and Corey were talking, and Turk told Corey that he was on some Bullshit. Turk knew that Corey wasn't being one hundred and the shit Corey was doing could cost them their lives. Corey knew at the end of the day it was his foolishness that got him in the situation back then. Now he was allowing his foolish pride to mislead him again. He knew that it was the penitentiary or the graveyard calling him.

Evil had just come from City Hall trying to get his liquor license back because one of his bartenders had served an underage female at his nightclub in Cleveland. The police were fucking with Evil every chance they got, but evil has gotten so sharp with it that he literally was ten steps ahead of them all the time. Monique was steady on the move from Cleveland to Columbus making sure everything was right at both beauty salons. Meagan and her family members were holding it down at their spots as well. Everybody was waiting for Wicked to come home. Big Moose got some good news from Paul Shapiro, his new appeal attorney. Big Moose found a loophole in his appeal. Paul Shapiro was the best appeal attorney in the State of Ohio. Wicked and Big Moose learned this together as both would spend hours in the law library trying to find something for Big Moose. Finally, Paul Shapiro told Big Moose that the sentencing guidelines had been changed prior to Big Moose's sentencing hearing back then. They discovered that Big Moose has an extra five years. Now Big Moose was going back to court to get resentenced. Wicked's life couldn't be better. He knew that his pops would be getting out in two more years. Wicked and Big Moose would be coming home right after each other. Now the only thing in Wicked's way was Corey's hot-headed ass. Wicked understood how the system was full of Coreys. This was something Wicked made clear to himself; that he would never let himself get caught back up in this cruel system that these white folks were making billions from homies in the inner cities. Wicked has become a man, but now he considers himself a businessperson with a plan. The penitentiary wouldn't ever see the likes of Wicked again. He loved his daughter and his mother so much to let them down.. The streets weren't ready for Wicked.

Nautica was furious as she tried repeatedly to get Corey to listen to her. She knew that Corey was on a suicide mission. In fact, everyone knew Corey was on a suicide mission. The odds were stacked against him, and he knew what he was facing but just like most young hot-headed niggas Corey wasn't trying to budge. Nautica did everything in her power to convince Corey that he should leave the shit alone. Corey, still in his feelings, kept telling Nautica and everyone else to let him handle what he had to handle. Finally, Nautica couldn't take Corey's foolish thinking anymore and flat out told Corey "NIGGA YOU GONE CHOOSE THE STREET LIFE OVER ME AND IF SO THEN FUCK YOU AND US!" Corey understood Nautica's pain and frustration. Corey and Turk had stopped talking. Turk couldn't deal with Corey's attitude towards the situation with Black. Turk found out from the streets that Corey was dead wrong for trying to fuck Black's bitch. Turk confronted Corey and the two of them had fallen out. Turk checked Corey and told him that real homies don't pull their homies into bullshit like this. Corey wasn't trying to hear anything Turk or anyone else had to say. He even sent word to Lancaster and told Wicked that the shit he was saying didn't hold any weight with him either. The bottom line is, Corey was out for revenge, and he had to have it at all costs. The graveyard or the penitentiary didn't mean shit to young Corey.

Chapter 11:

Friend or Foe

Monique and Meagan were talking and decided that it was time to have some good old-fashioned fun. Meagan, just like everyone else has been feeling the effects of all the drama. She couldn't remember the last time she or anybody in her close circle really had some fun lately. They all came together and decided that they were going to take all the kids to Disney World. Evil found out later and said he would pay for everything. Wicked was sad when he found out because he wanted to be part of that family affair. Everyone assured him that he would be with them in spirit. Meagan knew Wicked would be home soon and they would have plenty of family time. Little Mariah even knew her dad was coming home soon. Disney World was fun for grown people just as much for young people.

It was the best time that they've ever had in their entire lives. Everybody had a blast. The only person that wasn't there besides Wicked was Corey. No one has seen Corey and people started to worry about him. Meagan made sure Wicked got over a thousand pictures of the trip to Disney World. Wicked told Meagan that he wasn't going to miss any more family trips with her and his daughter, Meagan understood how Wicked felt.

Big Moose was still in court and Wicked didn't tell anybody about his pops court date. The only person that knew was Wicked's mother. Monique and Evil rented hall after hall for the next several months. The gang threw party after party and Robyn was glad to be back home and Selina was happy too. Meagan had run into Wicked's friend Black, and he was telling Meagan that he has a rap artist that made a song dedicated to Wicked's release. Black had a few up-and-coming rap artists, and he and Wicked had discussed potential business ventures together. However Wicked didn't envision Black putting a single out about him hitting the streets soon. The song was a big hit, and everyone was feeling it as the streets were on fire playing that song on all the radio stations. Wicked finally heard the song called "Back like I Never left." Black was putting it down and was staying true to his word with Wicked. Evil and Black had a good relationship. Black ran the largest rap label in Ohio, with some of the biggest artists under his wing. He was bringing everybody in the music game to Cincinnati and Columbus. He even had them going to Cleveland and Akron. All the big stars were fucking with Black. Black made sure that they knew about Wicked. Rick Ross, Drake, Lil Wayne, and Future just to name a few were fucking with Black heavily. Black had all types of music executives going to holla at Wicked in the joint. Wicked knew that the game was his and all he had to do was show up and show out. Corey heard the song for the first time and couldn't believe that Black was getting this much love. Corey was even mad at his sister Robyn for supporting that nigga. He knew he had to rock everybody to sleep so he could get close to Black and bring him down. Turk was the first person on Corey's list that he was going to rock to sleep.

Evil had not been in contact with Ashley since she filed a custody complaint a few years ago. Recently, he heard that Ashley wanted to talk to him, and he wondered why she was reaching out after all this time. Evil quickly thought about filing a restraining order against his baby momma Ashley. She is now married. Now Evil was trying to figure out what the fuck Ashley wanted with him now. Evil wasn't going to fool around with Ashley without his lawyer being present. However, Ashley convinced Evil to meet with her alone without any lawyers. They met at the Hard Rock Café in the arena district in the Short North of Columbus. Ashley's eyes teared up as she explained to Evil how her husband had touched their daughter Miracle. Ashley was shaking as she told Evil that she and Miracle had moved to Zanesville, Ohio to be with her grandmother. Evil couldn't stomach what he was hearing. Evil told Ashley to give him all the information she had on his bitch ass. His name is Melvin Thompson and he worked at Pepsi in Hilliard, Ohio. Evil knew he would deal with this joker, but knew he had to get it done quietly.

Turk and Alyson have been together for about nine months. They have a little spot in Dublin, Ohio out the way. Alyson just passed the bar and was going back to Ohio State to get her law degree. She has been offered a partner's position at Dan Orlosky's firm and she knew that was courtesy of Monique. Turk was learning a lot from Alyson like playing golf and eating white people's food. Turk always teased Alyson about the food she ate such as Hungarian Goulash and Alyson would tease Turk saying all he wanted was some fried chicken and pussy. Corey has been hanging out with Turk for a few weeks and Turk knew Corey was being extra nice for a reason. The two of them would play Madden like they used to, and they would shoot pool and hit the strip clubs up. Corey really did miss his homeboy Turk, but it was Turk who didn't miss Corey and his bullshit. Turk has told Corey that Robyn was throwing a get together and he should go. Everyone was gathered at the party, and the atmosphere was lively. Corey's presence among his old family and friends made him realize what he had been missing out on. However, Corey's mind was set on a mission, and he was determined to confront Black and knock his head off, or so he thought. It was all over the internet, Facebook, Instagram, you name it that Black has put together an all-star lineup that will be performing at one of his clubs in Cincinnati called PLATINUMS. Chris Brown, K Michelle, Future, and Gotti will be performing. Corey thought that would be the perfect time to catch Black slipping.

Wicked was heartbroken and couldn't believe the shit Evil was telling him. All Wicked kept saying was "Man that bitch ass nigga dead." Evil already knew what his brother was going to say and how he would feel. Wicked loved Miracle like he loves Mariah and was right there at the hospital when Ashley gave birth. In fact, Wicked was the only person at the hospital beside Evil, and he is her godfather.

Nautica texted Corey back and told him that she didn't want to meet with him because he was drunk. Nautica hasn't seen Corey in three weeks ever since he disrespected her and called her a nothing-ass bitch in front of their friends. Nautica was done with Corey, not knowing what to do, Corey begged and pleaded with Nautica to give him another chance. Corey had been going to a different strip club every night paying top dollars for some head and pussy. That shit was getting old, and Corey missed the way Nautica's lil short thick ass used to ride that dick. Nautica had Corey's nose wide open, and everybody knew it but him. Finally, Nautica agreed to meet Corey at their favorite Japanese food spot off 161. Corey kept trying to explain himself and his actions to Nautica and although Nautica was mad at Corey, she realized how much she missed her man. Nautica knew she wasn't about to give Corey any pussy or suck his dick. Once Corey knew he was dead on the pussy and head, he changed his entire attitude. Corey confided in Nautica and made the cardinal sin by letting his left hand know what the right hand was doing. Corey told Nautica that he was going to kill Black at the concert next Friday.

Nautica knew at that point there was no need to help him because she realized that he has a death certificate with his name on it. All she was going to do was make sure her name didn't get added to it. Nautica told

Corey that she wasn't ready to jump back into any relationship right now. She told Corey that they needed to think about what they really wanted from each other. She knew Corey was about to bring a lot of heat to her and the crew. She decided to holla at Robyn and tell her what her little brother was planning. Robyn quickly got word to Wicked and told him. Wicked not wanting to go there with his lil homie knew something has to be done before Corey blew shit up. Wicked contacted Evil and told Evil to reach out to Black and put this shit to rest for the last time. Wicked felt bad and he knew that this was the only thing to do. Turk sat and listened to Evil, and Black set the play up and everyone knew how Corey felt about them redbones. The night before the concert, Turk and Corey had a room at the Hyatt Hotel in Cincinnati. Corey was under the impression that Turk was going to help him trick Black away from everybody so Corey could blow his head off but what Corey didn't know was that Turk, Evil, and Black had found this redbone bitch to put it down on Corey.

Turk and Corey went to Christy's strip club in Cincinnati where the redbone bitch danced at. Nikki already was in on the play, and she knew who Corey was. So, she put the extra nasty walk and talk down on Corey. Just as everybody suspected, he fell for the bait. Nikki told Corey she wanted to fuck his brains out and they could go to the hotel. Corey being the pussy hound he was asked her if they could get live tonight. Nikki told Corey to pick her up as soon as she got off. As soon as they got inside the room, Nikki went straight to work. She started playing with Corey's dick even before he could pull it out. His dick was so hard that he told her he thought it was going to burst. Nikki made him lie down, pulled his pants off and licked his dick with her tongue concentrating only on the lining of his dick head. Corey was out of his mind. Nikki told Corey to hold on while she washed her pussy from dancing all night. She told Corey to keep that dick nice and hard. Corey knew he was about to beat that pussy up, so he grabbed the condom from his Gucci jean pocket and waited on Nikki. Just as she came out of the bathroom, she told Corey to lie flat on his back so she could ride that dick. As she walked towards the bed, she reached for her bag and pulled out the gun. Corey never saw the gun; he was busy thinking about this redbone bitch riding his dick. When Nikki said Corey look baby, he looked up at her and she shot him twice. Both bullets hit him right in the middle of his forehead killing him instantly. Then this bitch cut his dick off just in case. When the word hit the streets that young Corey aka Crazy C got killed, the shit was ugly. Wicked had promised Evil that he would handle the Melvin cat. Wicked had a white person he knew was a beast with explosives. Wicked gave Chris the info he needed to deal with Melvin. Chris learned about Melvin's work hours and within a few days, he had the car wired for sound. It was around 9:00 pm and Melvin had just got off work so he went to his car. As soon as he got in and turned the ignition, all that could be heard was a loud "boom" and the whole car went into the air. Before the car hit the ground it was nothing but a fireball. Nobody could recognize Melvin. He was burned to a crisp. Wicked and Evil were talking on Wicked's cell phone and Evil said to Wicked, "In this game, you never know if a muthafucka is a friend or a foe." Wicked said to Evil, "Love is nothing, but Loyalty is everything in this game."

Chapter 12:

Business 101

Big Moose had just arrived back at Lancaster, Wicked met his pops at the front gate. He has been waiting for his pops to get back for a month. Big Moose told his son everything that happened. Big Moose said the judge was so mad that he had to resentence him that his whole face turned red. Wicked and his pops both laughed at the judge turning red. Wicked couldn't have been happier. Wicked knew that it was time to get down to business. Shit was really looking good and Big Moose was coming home sooner than anybody knew. Wicked filled his pops in on the latest events that had unfolded while he was gone. Big Moose told his son that now everybody had to be strictly about business. Wicked made phone call after phone call. He was on a mission, and he needed his team to understand that everybody had to step their game up. Meagan hasn't seen Wicked more determined about his life, and he was focused on getting everybody's mind to be more business minded. Wicked understood that just making money was easy. However, it was what you did with the money that made all the difference. Therefore, Wicked made sure he educated his team to know how important it is to own shit.

Wicked sat down on visits with everybody; Selina and Robyn came together and Wicked made sure that they invested in all the local apartment buildings and rehab houses in the city. Wicked knew that buying a property would always generate money. He contacted his siblings in Cleveland and made sure they bought property too. His grandmother had gotten sick, so he made sure his family invested in nursing homes for the elderly. Wicked wasn't about to allow his grandmother or anybody in his family to be mistreated. Once Wicked felt that everybody was on their grind, he focused his attention on his newfound success. Black and Wicked never really discussed the details of Corey; they both knew that what was fully understood doesn't need further explanation. Plus, these two were just alike; they both have a woman that loved their dirty draws, and they shared the same vision and goals in life. When Black left Lancaster almost three years ago, he made a promise to Wicked that he would hold him down and ever since Black went home, he has kept his word. Wicked still couldn't believe that Black had one of his rap artists record the song about him. That song did numbers and Wicked knew he has a spot in the rap game. Wicked already knew his social status would make him a platinum-selling artist and Black knew this as well. It was a winning situation for the two to become partners. The concert was a tremendous success, and everybody was calling Black the new face of the rap game. All the local rap artists were trying to get along with Black and sign under his label. Black had the rap game on smash but he needed Wicked and Wicked needed him. The BET awards were coming, and Black has two artists up for the best new artist. On his part, he won the executive of the year award. Black thanked Wicked! Wicked saw his nigga Black on TV and knew at once that this was where he belonged. All the rapping ass Kats in Lancaster were on Wicked's neck. Wicked has been in the music room every day by himself, but he told Black that he would have the mixtape ready by the summer. Wicked knew he didn't have time to waste. The year came in and wicked smiled and said to Big Moose, next year is our big year homie!! In the meantime, Wicked teamed up with a few niggas at Lancaster. These dudes Wicked was fucking with were hot and the whole prison loved them. Wicked has never been a fool; he heard them rap and knew at once that he had to have them on a few songs they had recorded out to Black. Once Black got the song in his hand, he did his thing and history was made. Wicked and his niggas heard their music on other people MP3's. The nigga Black had put it down so their music could be bought on iTunes and off the Kiosk machines in every prison, but Wicked told Black he wanted to send his music to the feds and put his shit on Corlinks. Wicked was getting increasingly aggressive in the music game and all the people Wicked was fucking with in Lancaster were eating off the music they were selling. Wicked has a nigga in Lancaster that was putting the beats together so raw niggas on the streets were trying to fuck with the homie they called KT. Evil has been in Miami and Houston for the past few months. He hadn't really been to Ohio and couldn't make the BET awards. However, he saw Black and the rest of the crew in the front row. Evil knew that it was a matter of time before Wicked would be on the cover of XXL or Hip Hop Weekly. Evil has always loved Wicked's music. He used to tell Wicked that one day you gone have this rap game in a choke like Face, Pac, Biggie, and Jay Z but presently, Evil was dealing with some personal issues. Ever since Ashley told him about the Melvin nigga touching Miracle, he had to move Ashley into one of his houses but what Evil did that made him a true boss was he had Monique talk to Ashley. Evil asked Monique to talk to Ashley and give her some game about how shit really goes. Monique never really liked Ashley, not that she was jealous of Ashley. It was just that Monique never liked lazy bitches. Monique has pretty much known that Evil and Ashley met on some young dumb shit and Evil has fucked around and got Ashley pregnant. Monique finally had the bitch right in front of her, so she asked Ashley what she wants out of life. Ashley looked at Monique with rage in her eyes and said, "whatever I want I don't need your help getting it." But what Ashley did not realize was that Monique has already been battle tested when dealing with females way worse than Ashley. Monique told Ashley that she wasn't going to waste either of their time so Monique simply told Ashley to learn how to respect herself and people would respect her. Ashley knew Monique was right.

The shit with Corey had people dealing with mixed emotions; some knew what really went down but some didn't and the people on the outside looking in felt like nothing has been done to revenge Corey. This made Turk look bad. Everybody knew how close Turk and Corey had been. So, sometimes Turk would be in traffic, and some dudes and bitches would mean mug him. Muthafuckas were even sending death threats to Turk, but Turk knew the shit would work itself out, so he hoped. Turk told Alyson that he didn't want to smoke a muthafucka, but he would if he had to. But Turk had bigger things going for himself. Turk was TT's cousin and Wicked wanted to spend more time with TT. Ever since Wicked met TT, she has been on his mind. TT has made a name for herself in the porn industry but more importantly, TT has a brand and a market. TT knew how to make money and she knew pussy was the oldest money maker on planet earth. She has over five hundred films she has done and all the bitches in the porn game were trying to be like her. TT has even started producing her own movies and this is where Wicked came in. Wicked knew that if they could collab, he could have her signed under his entertainment label, and it would be on the floor. Wicked knew that TT wouldn't come at a cheap price plus Wicked really respected TT's mind and wanted to work with her.

All Wicked wanted to do is have a sit down with Ms. TT so the meeting finally took place in the visiting room at Lancaster. After five minutes of talking to Wicked, TT knew she wanted to hook up with him. She told Wicked that if she agreed to sign with him, she would still control sixty percent of her porn money and business. Wicked quickly agreed to her price. The two shook hands and it was history in the making. Once TT was able to set up shop, she quickly set up a magazine company in Columbus to promote homegrown talent. Before she knew it, bitches from as far as Tennessee were trying to get in where they fit in. Wicked was excited about everything TT was doing. Black even reached out to Wicked and informed him that he was going to use TT and some of her bitches to do music videos. Business was booming on every level and Wicked remembered what his pops had told him on that first visit by himself. Big Moose told the young eighteen-year-old Wicked "if you take care of your business, your business will take care of you." Wicked never forgot those words. In fact, he never forgot shit his pops ever told him. He loved his pops and knew he deserved a second chance at life. Wicked was going to make sure his pops was going to be good from the first day he came home up until his last day on this earth. The day had finally come and Wicked's mixtape was complete. Black was excited to get his hands on it so he could get it popping on all the airways. It was a masterpiece, and all the tracks were on point. Once the mixtape hit the streets, it was official that Wicked made it in the rap game.

Evil told Wicked that he was going to start being more engaged in his clubs. Evil was on a mission himself, he wanted to open as many food spots throughout Ohio as he could. Evil learned a lot from the business class he had taken; he learned how to market. He knew that eventually he would franchise his name and help young black people start their own businesses. Meagan was doing her thing and she had opened several beauty salons on damn near every side of town in Columbus. Everywhere you went, you would see one of Meagan's beauty salons. Meagan used her real estate experience to buy houses and apartment buildings in Columbus and Cleveland. She was a force to be reckoned with when it came to the real estate game; Meagan was second to none. She hired Alyson as her corporate attorney to deal with all her legal endeavors. Meagan was a highly sought-after realtor in Columbus, but her true powerhouse move came when she teamed up with Evil. Together, they launched a chain of soul food restaurants that drew in a diverse crowd of diners, from local celebrities to politicians. Their collaboration was a huge success, and soon their restaurants became a staple of Ohio's dining scene. The food was off the hook and everyone loved not just the food but also the service. Wicked knows what he has in Meagan and Meagan knows what she has in Wicked. Now all Wicked had to do is keep everybody on the same page until he got home. Robyn visited Wicked because she said she needed to talk to him. Wicked already knew it was about Corey. Robyn sat in front of Wicked with tears in her eyes while talking about how hard it has been for her to deal with losing her little brother. Wicked knew that this day would come, but he just didn't know when. All Wicked could say to Robyn was "What were we supposed to do when you knew Corey was going to send people to jail or the graveyard?" Robyn admitted back then that Corey was lost and out of control. She even told Wicked that she thought Corey was going to kill her for siding with Wicked. Wicked told Robyn that at the end of the day, something bad was going to happen to Corey. Wicked asked Robyn if she wanted something bad to happen to her or another family member because of what Corey was doing. Wicked finally got through to her and she hugged him and left. He watched her leave and said boy ol' boy, I wish I could fuck her right now. Wicked was a little concerned about Turk and how he was adjusting. He had asked Evil to keep a closer eye on Turk. Evil told Wicked that he would have him run the strip club "WICKEDS" in Cleveland. Evil told Wicked that Turk was a natural-born playa, so he should do great with the strip club scene. Turk was cool with it since he hasn't been doing shit but chilling with Alyson. So he was more than willing to get his feet wet. Turk knew that he was chosen to do this job for a reason, so failure wasn't a choice on his part. All Turk thought about becoming was the next important thing, and he wasn't going to let anybody stop him. He really understood that this shit was strictly business.

Chapter 13:

Under Surveillance

Dan Orlosky had his secretary contact Monique. He received a tip from one of his friends on the police force that the FBI was investigating Evil again. Monique knew that ever since she proved her loyalty to Dan Orlosky, he owed her his life. Monique met Dan Orlosky at a quiet little restaurant on the outskirts of Washington Courthouse. Monique knowing Dan figured this had to be important, so she told him to cut straight to the chase. He told Monique that Evil hired this young girl named April to run the bar and the bartenders but there was a problem. She was arrested a month ago with some cocaine and pills. The feds took advantage of her situation being a young single parent and told her to work for them and help gather some information against Evil and they would make her arrest go away. Monique was thankful for Dan Orlosky, she knew that this was vital information that could save her and Evil. Monique hugged Dan and told him that she appreciated everything he had done for her. Monique made sure Mrs. Orlosky got fifty thousand dollars towards her school program and Mrs. Orlosky loved Monique. Evil couldn't believe that the feds were back on his trail. He figured that he has been dotting all his I's and crossing all his Ts. Nevertheless, Evil understood how the feds worked and couldn't afford to have them set him up. Nautica had been assigned to get close to April and find out where she lived. April was a loner and really didn't like to go places and this made it difficult for Nautica to get any information on April. So, Nautica decided to come up with a story that she and her boyfriend were going through some rough times. Nautica knew that if April has a heart, she would find out. Nautica put on a show and convinced April that her boyfriend was beating her ass every night. April told Nautica to go to the police, but Nautica reminded April that the police wouldn't do shit until she was close to death or dead altogether. April finally gave in and allowed Nautica to stay with her for a couple of weeks. While Nautica was living with April, she made up all kinds of stories about Evil. Nautica painted a picture of Evil that made April really hate Evil. One day Nautica came home and told April that she had to tell her something. Nautica told April that she had to give her word that she wouldn't say anything, or she could die. April was terrified for Nautica and gave Nautica her word that this was between the two of them. Nautica told April that Evil raped her and was making her sell drugs to strange men. She had April hanging on to every word and April began crying, saying how can we take this piece of shit down? Nautica said we must work together and trust one another. That's when April said, "the FBI made me wear a wire to work to try to get Evil's voice on wire saying anything incriminating." April thought Nautica was really going to help her out and even told Nautica that she was arrested.

Evil and Monique listened to Dan Orlosky as he explained to Evil the importance of his paperwork. Dan Orlosky and Evil had this talk over a million times about Evil overspending. Evil couldn't process how the banks and credit cards went hand and hand. No matter how much Evil made, he always either bought too much or had too much. It didn't matter if it was Evil having an extra ten million in liquor or getting too many home improvement loans from different banks. Evil always made the government question his assets. Now it was Evil and his extra unknown bank accounts that had the IRS on his heels. Monique always wondered why Evil often needed extra money. Dan Orlosky basically told Evil that he better stop at every red light in the world. Evil heard Dan Orlosky loud and clear. Monique understood that the IRS was watching their every move.

Black had recently visited his accountant, who had sent him a text message informing him that the IRS had paid a visit to his office and inquired about scrutinizing the financial records of his record company, BLACK DIAMOND. After hearing this, Black called Peter Kindle about it. Peter Kindle assured Black that their numbers were exactly right. But the problem was that a couple of Black's rappers have been investigated by the gang task force. This is how Black got pulled into this and now the feds have BLACK DIAMOND RECORDS on their hit list. Wicked told Black that he knew about this shit because muthafuckas in the joint were running their mouths. Wicked's name has been tossed across the compound at Lancaster and he was even placed in segregation for investigation about some rival rap groups on the streets that mentioned Wicked's name in one of their songs. Wicked was eventually released from the hole after twenty-one days. Black told Wicked that dudes were hating on them, but that shit wasn't going to stop them or slow them down. Black used all the hating they were getting as fuel to inspire him and his team to rise above everybody.

April was busy telling Nautica everything the federal agent she was working for told her. Nautica was shocked to hear how much information April had on Evil. April told Nautica that she heard Evil telling someone on the phone she believed was a female, "Don't worry about shit, you know I'm going to take care of you and the baby." Nautica couldn't believe this shit. All Nautica kept thinking was his bitch ass got another baby behind Monique's back. April even told Nautica that the woman was married but the bombshell was April knew Evil played a part in Corey's death. Nautica made sure April didn't make any sudden moves to the feds with that information about Corey. Nautica convinced April to help her catch Evil in a drug transaction. She tricked April into thinking that she knew Evil was doing a drug transaction in two days. April thought she and Nautica would secretly record the drug transaction with their cell phones then they would take that video to the federal agent that April was working for. Nautica explained the whole play to Evil. Evil told Black what Nautica had told him, Black knew that the feds were fucking with him for a reason and now he knew why. Black agreed with Evil that this bitch April had to go, so Evil set the play in motion. Nautica and April were going to record the whole thing right after April met with the federal agent. The two women made sure they had everything ready and Nautica ask April for the last time, "Are you sure nobody else knows about this?" April assured Nautica that the federal agent she met with didn't know anything about it. Nautica made sure that they both drove their own cars but she had April follow her to a spot in Delaware, Ohio. Nautica told April where to park so she wouldn't get spotted. April parked her black Lexus behind a liquor store facing the building where the drug deal was supposed to take place. April saw some bright light from a truck approaching her. April didn't know what to do at that moment. She tried to start her Lexus and back out of the little alley she was in, however it was too late. The truck pressed on the accelerator and smashed poor little April into the brick wall. Shortly after, two men dressed in all-black emerged from the truck with nine millimeters displayed. You could see the silencers at the end of the gun as they approached the Lexus. April was hit with at least twenty shots that covered her entire body. The men grabbed her phone and other personal belongings. The federal agent April was meeting was the first on the scene. She is a ten-year veteran on the force and hated street thugs. Her name is Vivian Goldberg, and she has a sister that had a black man who treated her badly. Vivian never liked street thugs for that reason. Her sister's boyfriend who was a street thug went to prison and made her sister bring him heroin. Eventually, her sister got arrested for doing that and lost her kids. It has been personal for Vivian ever since. The media was all over this shooting. All the people living in that community kept saying was "Nothing like this has ever happened before in this community." Nobody seemed to know anything about April's death. The only thing people kept saying was she was a loner and stayed to herself. The feds interviewed Nautica hard over the next few days and Monique quickly pushed Dan Orlosky on the feds. Nautica knew she would go through strict scrutiny, and she was prepared for the feds. Nautica never spoke to the feds without Dan or someone from his firm present. The feds turned the heat up on Black; it wasn't a secret that Black was dealing with a lot of people in the street. Wicked's name was at the top of the fed's list and Black kept telling Wicked that it was important for him to chill. Wicked was on his C-Murder shit sending a hell of videos out from a cell phone camera. All those videos Wicked was sending out were being played on YouTube and Facebook. All the streets kept talking about was Wicked's videos. Meagan was being harassed by the feds constantly.

The fed wasn't the only one turning up the heat; Monique also heard everything from Nautica, but Monique had already been suspicious of Evil's recent behavior. Monique noticed that when Evil went to Miami, he wouldn't return a lot of her calls. He would always claim that he either didn't have any service or that his phone had probably died. Monique never forgot who Evil was, she knew that this nigga of hers was a sucka for a bad bitch. She always tried to give this nigga, Evil the benefit of the doubt, but he would try to play Monique for a fool too many times. Evil knew when he first started fucking with the Cuban bitch that she was trouble. Not only was the bitch drop dead gorgeous, but she was also married. Evil had met Rachelle a few years back and used to visit her at her job all the time. Her family owned one of the best Cuban restaurants in Miami. Evil remembered the first time he fucked Rachelle; once he had fucked her, it was over. Rachelle was pregnant, and she led her husband to believe it was his baby. However Evil and Rachelle, both knew it was Evil's baby. After a paternity test was carried out on Evil and the little boy, the results came back with a 99.99 percent match, confirming that the child was indeed his. Evil knew that he had to take responsibility for his actions while maintaining a positive relationship with the woman and hoping that Monique would never find out. Sometimes Evil used to say things would be better if I just told Monique in the beginning but it was too late now. Rachelle already had the baby and Evil was indeed the father. Monique hired a private investigator to fly to Miami and investigate Mrs. Rachelle's background. Evil felt the pressure coming from Rachelle, she had become extremely aggressive with her list of commands and demands. Evil had promised her that they were going to be together, and he was leaving Monique for her. The only problem was Evil had no intention of leaving Monique. Rachelle had every intention of leaving her husband. In fact, Rachelle had already moved out of their house and was living in an apartment for a few months. Rachelle was waiting for Evil so they could move to Orlando Florida; that's what Evil had promised Rachelle. Now Evil knew that Rachelle wanted answers and wanted them now. Monique had a feeling that Evil was doing something with all the extra money he was using. She thought he had developed a gambling habit but quickly erased that thought. Monique knew Evil didn't like losing in anything, so gambling was out of the question. Monique knew in her gut that Evil has another woman on the side, but she had no idea a baby was involved. Meagan was running at a steady pace on the treadmill as she told Monique that Evil always had a trick dick. Both women laughed as they knew Evil's weakness when it came to women. Robyn hasn't exercised in God knows how long and it showed. Selina couldn't talk about anyone as all the women talked and joked about Selina's ghetto booty. Even Wicked's two sisters have decided to come and hang out and this was the first time in a long time that all these women were together.

The whole crew was on their A-game when the heat from the feds had slowed down. However, everybody knew that shit could change at the drop of a hat. Wicked was so excited that he was down to six months that he couldn't sleep. The streets were buzzing about Wicked's release and Black kept trying to convince Wicked to let him throw a welcome home party. On the other hand, Wicked was sticking to his game plan. All Wicked wanted to do was come home as quietly as possible. Wicked's brother Willis had come back to Cleveland. Willis had been back in Cleveland for the past two months. Willis and his wife Summer have been divorced now for ten months and Willis was still practicing Islam and still tried to convert any and everybody willing to listen. Wicked was glad that he and his brother were spending time together. Willis hasn't seen his little brother or his pops for at least three years, but both Wicked and Big Moose were pleased to have Willis back in their lives. Willis told his brother that he has his back, and he was home for good. Wicked knew he was going to need Willis to help him rise back to the top. Only this time, Wicked wouldn't allow the streets to bring him down. He understood that Hollywood is the most addictive drug in the world.

Chapter 14:

Celebrity Status

TT was back in town fresh from a tour and she was the hottest thing on the internet. Her book has sold over a million copies. TT had the shit on lock when it came to pussy, power, and celebrity status. Her book titled "Sex, Secrets, and Lies," was the talk of the porn world, and every female in the world was addicted to her book like a crack addict is addicted to crack. TT had niggas talking shit about her because she was exposing niggas that were paying top dollar for pussy. She also had the women going crazy because she touched on the main topic that everyone was interested in, "Does size really matter?" TT had the radio stations, talk shows, and TMZ all trying to interview her but what really made her an instant success story was how she rose to the top from being at the bottom. Nobody could tell a story like TT; she had every female respecting her gangster as far as how she discovered the power of pussy. TT learned at an early age that men would do "anything" for that "special thing." TT said she remembered when she was twelve years old, this old ass man that lived next door used to pay her to walk to the store for him. TT said that this old ass nigga only wanted to see her ass and watch her walk. She understood that walking in a certain way and talking in a certain way could get her nearly anything from a nigga. Once TT lost her virginity, it was on and popping. Niggas from everywhere went wherever TT was doing her thing at. None of this news about TT was more satisfying for anyone other than Wicked. As Wicked watched TT on TV and listened to her on the radio, she always mentioned Wicked. The entire world knew that Wicked and TT had joined forces. Wicked had just released his rap label and Black promoted the party. Evil made sure everybody has first-class and VIP treatment. The rap game has been taken by storm and young Wicked, courtesy of Ms. TT and Black was a force to be reckoned with. Wicked sat back and understood what was waiting for him on the other side of the fence after spending nine and a half years in jail. Nobody was more focused or more determined to succeed than Wicked himself. Time was steadily moving, and it was getting close to crunch time for Wicked. Meagan came to see Wicked because she needed him to know that Monique was about to hit Evil in his pocket. Meagan went on to explain to Wicked what exactly had happened. After Wicked heard the whole story, he told Meagan not to get involved but to allow Monique and Evil to work their problems out. Evil and Monique had come to an understanding and Monique told Evil that he had to give her a good reason she shouldn't take him up top. Evil offered to give Monique the world but what Monique wanted was for Evil to fly to Miami and cut all ties with his baby momma. Evil knew he didn't have a choice. Despite all his foolishness, Evil really did love Monique and Monique knew that Evil fucked up big time. Monique loves Evil but wasn't going to put up with any more of his bullshit. However, the damage had been done. Back in Miami, Rachelle's husband knew everything.

Lancaster was in an uproar because Wicked had just been named best rapper in the latest Hip Hop Weekly. The COs were even going crazy trying to get Wicked to sign photos and shit. The whole DRC was calling this nigga Big Meech. Wicked understood that he had shit in the choke from behind bars. Now he thought to himself all he had to do was get back out there. Wicked had been the voice behind damn nearly everything that went on in the streets. Everyone knew Wicked was still calling the shots; the feds, the gang task force, the Columbus detectives, and even the DRC knew who Wicked was and more importantly, Wicked knew who he was. Wicked reached celebrity status and hasn't even walked on any stage in America yet. This was unheard of for somebody to achieve what Wicked did in the joint and what was even more crazy is how he was able to put niggas on from the joint before they had even gone home. Wicked had niggas featuring on his songs and had niggas put out their own mixtapes. All this was done from the music room at Lancaster. Niggas on the streets were feeling Wicked and not to mention all the music videos he sent to the streets from the joint. The shit had Black getting pulled over nearly every day. The police have been on Black, and it was so tuff he couldn't drive from streetlight to streetlight without getting stopped. Black was the standard for any successful black man. He would drive down the streets of Cincinnati in Maserati, Lambos, Aston Martins, you name it. The nigga would be with all types of ball players from NBA players to niggas in the NFL. Black's net worth was estimated to be around 40 million dollars. Black was ready to achieve hood legend status. Niggas from Black's hood were trying to get a statue built in front of their projects of the nigga Black.

TT has been back in town for a few weeks now. She was putting it down and her magazine was selling off every store shelf. The magazine is called "Finer Things." It is basically a self-help guide to empower young black women who have a vision. TT really didn't care what color a bitch was if she was trying to get that almighty dollar. She was in the works with a local film agency that wanted to do a documentary on Wicked's life. The filmmakers had contacted TT with this information, and she told Wicked. Wicked wasn't sure if he wanted to do it but TT told Wicked that it was a win for everybody. Black even told Wicked that the film company wanted to shoot his release from the parking lot and follow him home. Wicked couldn't believe how much power was being put in his hands. All he could think about was niggas like Master P and Fifty Cent. Wicked knew now that money is nothing but power is everything. Now all he had to do is gain this power he knew he could obtain it. Wicked needed the streets and the streets needed Wicked. TT mastered the music game, and she had her girls performing in every music video known to man. She was the executive producer in most of the videos and she was even shooting xxx movies.

Wicked's brother Willis was finding his groove since he came back. He started a chain of laundromats and gas stations. Willis used to move a lot of work before he had gotten set up by some New York nigga he was fucking with. Willis had shit on smash back then and Wicked always admired his brother. When everybody heard Willis was a Muslim, they couldn't believe it. All everybody used to say when they heard Willis is a Muslim was "All that nigga trying to fake it till he makes it." Willis knew that his life couldn't be defined as a street legend, so he did what he was supposed to do. The nigga got to the feds and educated himself. This nigga took any and every course the feds had to offer. He always knew that you could take a nigga out of the ghetto, but you couldn't take the ghetto out of a nigga. Wicked remembered the first time he heard his brother was a Muslim, he couldn't believe it. Wicked has always known his brother to be a real live street nigga that sold crack for a living but what nobody realized was that Willis had connections all over the world. After Wicked really started to pay attention to his brother's movements, he knew that Willis had some Arab muthafuckas on his team that loved his ass. These Arab niggas had so much dope and money, it was crazy. Wicked never doubted that his brother was smart but Wicked had an idea his brother was fucking with muthafuckas like them Arabs. Willis and them Arabs had stores and gas stations everywhere. Willis made sure he had shit nearly on every corner in almost every city. The craziest shit was how much power Willis had. Wicked said that his brother must have some type of rank in that Islam shit because muthafuckas did what Willis told them to do. Willis is sharp and Wicked loved his brother.

Black had just returned from Vegas. One of his rap artists had a pool party for his album release. Black and South Side Records were beefing because South Side Record's CEO blamed Black for stealing one of his artists in some contract controversy. Black's record company was being sued by this nigga's lawyer for ten million. The news was all over the TV and all over the radio stations. People were weighing their comments as to what they believed about Black and what they believed about South Side Records. The problem is Black's name had a reputation connected to it that involved some behind-the-scenes gangster shit. Some people felt like Black, and his boys would force rap artists to sign under his label or they couldn't rap with anybody. Comments like that made people unsure about Black's reputation. Especially when two summers ago Black was arrested and questioned about a homicide that one of his boys was alleged to have committed in Memphis. After investigating Black, he was later cleared of any wrongdoing. Nevertheless, this has always carried a black cloud over Black's record company and now he was being sued for extortion and breach of contract. Black's girl Kesha's uncle worked directly with the Mayor of Cincinnati. Kesha had her uncle get the lawsuit dropped.

Wicked and Black along with Evil all talked, Wicked was on his cell phone talking to Black and Evil. The three of them discussed how important things had to tighten up. Wicked felt like by him being on the outside and looking inward, he saw shit they couldn't see. They all agreed that shit had to get better, but they also agreed that too many people had access to them. Wicked, already feeling like he was a private person, kept stressing to Evil and Black the reason he doesn't like crowds. Wicked reminded Evil that it was the after party that sent him to prison. Wicked always thought that if he had just listened to Meagan back then, he wouldn't be in prison now. So, before they all hung up, they made a deal that from here on out, nobody could have full access to any of them.

Evil knew he had to tell Wicked that he was going to Miami. He finally told Wicked himself everything that was going down between him and Rachelle. Wicked told him to dump that bitch and leave her alone. What Wicked knew of Monique is that he understood she would be in Evil's corner over any other bitch. Evil boarded the plane headed to South

Beach. All he could think about was Rachelle's face once he told her he wouldn't be moving to Orlando with her and their son. Evil got to the hotel that he had booked a room in, after unloading his luggage, he made the call and told Rachelle to meet him at TRUTH's, one of their favorite food spots. Evil waited for about ten minutes before Rachelle arrived. She looked very distraught, and Evil knew something was wrong. Rachelle came right out and said Evil, my husband knows everything and he has taken our son. Evil's heart sank to his stomach because he knew her husband had Columbian drug connections, and that meant he had soldiers on deck. Evil couldn't understand; how in the fuck did her husband find out? Rachelle explained to Evil that her sister overheard one of their conversations and told her husband, so her husband had her apartment bugged. Rachelle said her husband said that she would never see her son again and that you are a dead man. Evil knew he couldn't afford to go to war with this man. He knew he had to figure out a way to handle this shit before it got ugly. Before Evil left Miami, he tried to contact Rachelle's husband, but he was nowhere to be found. Evil knew at that point that he had to sleep with one eye open. He thought to himself, this was the last thing he needed. He knew the feds and everybody else would be all over him once the shit hit the fan. Evil was worried and there was nothing he could do about it except take this man head-on. So he started making phone calls to prepare for the battle coming his way. For the first time in a long time, Evil wished he had Wicked by his side right now.

Chapter 15:

War Ready

Wicked sat attentively and listened to his father, Big Moose, explain to him the significance of the upcoming months. Big Moose knew it was his duty to help his son focus on the big picture. Wicked had arranged for all his siblings to come and visit him. Wicked's mind was in attack mode. The two books he loved to read were (THE ART OF WAR AND FORTY-EIGHT LAWS OF POWER), and they were like the bible to Wicked. The more Wicked read those books the more focused he felt. Big Moose and Wicked spent as much time together as they could. Big Moose was so insightful for his son. Big Moose understood that he couldn't allow his son to go back into society unprepared. He always gave Wicked knowledge on any topic, but the main thing Big Moose kept preaching to his son was the exact same message Paul the (Apostle) in the bible preached. Big Moose constantly reminded Wicked, "When you were a child, you did childish things, but when you became a man, you put away all the childish things." He made sure his son knew that nobody in life was going to give him shit. Big Moose always told Wicked that there are two types of people in this world. Wicked had heard all his pops quotes and knew them by heart. So, when his pops said there are two types of people in this world, Wicked finished the statement by saying "Pops, it's homies that make shit happen and then there are dudes who wait on shit to happen." Basically, Wicked knew that the way he saw it was dudes be faking and dudes that be talking. Wicked loved Big Moose a lot and his dad knew his son was ready to hit those streets and never look back. It has been a long time since so many people were expecting one person's arrival. Wicked had jokingly made a comment one day to his pops and said, "Pops, sometimes I feel like the Pope or Jesus Christ," but it was true because everyone was waiting on Wicked. All Wicked's siblings had come to visit him but Wicked made his brothers come first and then his sisters. Wicked flat out told his brothers that they had to be ready mentally more than anything else. Wicked made sure his sisters knew that their lives were going to be different, and that they would be taken care of. Wicked made sure they knew their kids would be good too after each visit. His siblings knew that Wicked was focused and ready to take on his responsibilities. Nobody was more impressed than Wicked's mother because she has watched her son turn into a man right before her eyes. Tina knew Wicked was ready to be a father and a provider. Little Mariah has felt nothing but unconditional love from her father. Meagan loved Wicked and knew within herself that her man was a man amongst boys. She couldn't wait to get her hands on Wicked. Black has finally shaken South Side Records. He was moving and grooving again. His rap artists were all playing their positions and they knew that to take their own personal status to platinum level, they had to sharpen up. Black said he had to thank Wicked because Wicked had him on his A game.

It has been almost five years since Wicked saw Mrs. Patterson. She had come to visit Wicked back when he was filing for his advance release. Mrs. Patterson is the mother of James whom Wicked had killed back then. This was her second time coming to visit Wicked. The first time she came, it was very awkward for both. It was Wicked's mother who arranged the visit back then. But this time, it was all Wicked's doing. He has been sending Mrs. Patterson gifts for her birthdays and holidays.

Wicked knew that to have peace and closure in this situation, he had to get forgiveness from Mrs. Patterson. Wicked's brother Willis had run into Big Tone last summer and made sure Big Tone wasn't on no bullshit, but Big Tone pretty much knew how the shit went down that night. Big Tone contacted Wicked and told him that he is salty and his lil brother got killed but he knew Wicked did what he had to do. However, none of that shit really mattered to Wicked except James' mother's forgiveness. Wicked explained to Mrs. Patterson the events that unfolded that night and did his best to assure her that he was not the monster people made him out to be. In fact, Wicked convinced her that he didn't even know James at the time the incident happened. Mrs. Patterson believed that Wicked didn't even know James at the time the incident happened. She thanked him for the things he has been doing for her over the years. Mrs. Patterson has another younger son that was on the visit and Wicked made sure he had all the downloads he wanted from any rapper. Wicked knew he has done the right thing by making amends with Mrs. Patterson. He told Big Moose that he has done exactly what he had told him to do. Now Wicked said for these next few months, he was going to finish his mixtape so it would be ready by the time he went home. Things got serious for Wicked, and he understood that it was up to him to make it or break It. Failure didn't even fit in Wicked's life. All the home boyz that Wicked was fucking with in Lancaster, Wicked had them in the studio going in on their mixtapes as well. Young Wicked's plan was to not only have his mixtape done but all his homie" mixtapes done also. This would really kill the rap game and Wicked knew it.

Nothing seemed too big or too small for TT. She went at everything like it was her last day on earth. TT's motto was, "Why not do it right now…." She opened her own clothing store for women off Livingston Ave. She sold all kinds of sexy ass clothes that bitches went crazy over. Street thugs would be in there trying to buy shit for their girls. TT's best-seller was the Victoria Secret (PINK) lingerie. TT knew she would have to expand. The only thing that mattered to her was dead presidents. Turk had decided that he wanted in on some of the action. Turk gave TT a proposition and told her he would invest his money in her xxx movies. Turk told TT that he was trying to be the black Hugh Hefner for real. Turk even told TT that he would do movies or whatever it took to get his face and name out there. TT liked Turk and knew she could use his young, sexy, athletic body. Plus, TT found Turk to be a fine young thug. TT and Black discussed their usual business. She mentioned Turk to Wicked and he said, "Fuck it. If the nigga is trying to get his status up, then let him." Wicked reminded TT to stay sharp and stay on her A game. TT knew that Wicked was softer than a white man's dick buying pussy for the first time. She felt what Wicked was saying to her, but she felt like she was ten steps ahead of Wicked. Black made sure he stayed in contact with Wicked daily. Willis was doing his thing and had his Arab homie riding with him. Evil has finally surfaced from the shadows but he wasn't doing a lot of moving around. The crew felt like Evil might be involved in some heavy shit because he has distanced himself from everybody. Even Monique knew Evil wasn't telling her everything, though Evil told Monique that it was officially over with him and Rachelle. Nobody knew that Evil was a wanted man. Evil got back to Ohio and made it his duty to have shit ready for Wicked's arrival. The only thing that mattered to Evil was Wicked coming home to everything he was supposed to have and then some. Wicked stood in the music room and told all his people that they had just delivered a classic. The whole prison was on fire talking about the mixtape. Even the COs were feeling that shit. Wicked watched the crowd as he did song after song. Wicked knew in his mind that this shit felt so good being on stage performing in front of a crowd. This was good practice for Wicked and he loved the challenge. The word got out and soon Black had the official mixtape; he did in fact put together a bad muthafucka. Now all everybody could do was wait for the drop date. That was the day Wicked would be coming home and it was only eighty days away.

Chapter 16:

Final Thoughts

Evil knew that he had to get his troops in order. He thought to himself, I can't allow this shit between me and Rachelle's husband to interfere with Wicked's coming home party. All Evil kept thinking was he had to be on top of his game just in case the Columbian muthafucka came his way. Evil was aware that he was facing a life-or-death situation. Now Evil needed to protect Monique and everybody else in a couple of months. Wicked told his pops that he was going to take his life and family to places they couldn't even imagine. Wicked knew it was important for him to reflect on his life. All Wicked and Big Moose did daily was go over their game plan. All of them in the joint always talked about the things they were going to do once they got out. However, ninety-nine percent of the homies didn't have an effective game plan. Big Moose pounded in Wicked's head that if you do not plan, then you might as well plan to fail. Big Moose wasn't about to allow his son to fail. He understood that if Wicked went home and failed, then that meant he failed as well. The stakes were too high and both Big Moose and Wicked knew their family needed them and they needed their family. The ol' heads at Lancaster always told Wicked what to expect once he got home. Wicked used to always wonder how in the fuck could they leave and be right back within thirty days in some cases. Wicked would listen to what they had to say, plus he was aware of how the system was designed to keep a homie down and out. Nobody expected Wicked to come to the joint and educate himself the way he did. Wicked had authored an article for the Columbus Dispatch explaining how this legal system was designed to keep the black man down. The DRC had tried to lock Wicked up back then. Big Moose was extremely proud of how Wicked had overcome the system. Now it was time to show everybody what a success story looks like. The only thing Wicked kept stressing to all his people on the outside was don't allow anything you got going on in y'all personal lives to jeopardize anything the family is trying to do. Wicked was aware of all the shit Black's record company has been going through. He also knew about the problems Evil was having so Wicked made sure they knew everybody has a duty to protect the next man or woman.

Wicked was granted permission to meet with the movie crew, and the production team that would be shooting the documentary on his release. The name of the production team is Premiere Movies. They have produced a number of short films, which were largely trendy as well, however this would be their biggest event yet and the production crew was excited to get this right. They explained to Wicked exactly what to expect and how things would be done. Wicked was fascinated by just the thought of his face being on the big screen. He knew that it was Black that had convinced him to do this. Never in a million years did Wicked think he would be doing something like this. Wicked always said that he didn't want anybody to know when he was coming home. He was afraid the feds and fuck boyz in the streets would be trying to watch his every move. Those thoughts and worries made Wicked understand what he was up against. The main thing Wicked was concerned about was his mother, daughter, and Meagan's safety. He listened to the production team as they showed him some footage of what they had envisioned. He saw what they were intending to do, and he loved it. They had Wicked looking like a movie star. This had Wicked already thinking of BET, VH1, Grammys, and any other award shows he could be a part of. Wicked and TT had already discussed what her role was going to be in this documentary. Wicked wanted TT and her girls on deck doing their thing behind Wicked once he got to the club Evil set up for him. Wicked even told the production team that he wanted a piece done on his mother separately. He wanted his mother's face out there to show what a strong black woman looks like. Of course, Tina wasn't down with it at first but Wicked and everybody else talked her into it. The production team told Wicked they would see him on February 10th. They made sure Wicked knew that he had to be ready to start shooting by nine that morning. After bidding farewell to the production team, Wicked felt a sense of excitement and anticipation. He knew that their paths would cross again, and the next time they did, he would be embarking on a new journey. All Wicked could do from that point on was to work out. He ran the tracks every day. He also did pull-ups, push-ups, dips, and everything else he could think of to try to make the days go by. Big Moose had to kick it with him as much as he could just so Wicked wouldn't go crazy. Wicked couldn't even sleep anymore. The days couldn't go by fast enough for him. Black and Evil both assured Wicked that everything was in order.

Now everybody had to just wait until February 10th.

Night turned to days and days turned to nights as Wicked sat in his cell looking out his window. February 10th was right there and Wicked could smell it. Big Moose and Wicked were in the yard walking the track one day and Big Moose said to Wicked "Man it's cold out here, I'm going in." Wicked said jokingly to his pops, "Damn old man, you don't have no blood in your body." Both men laughed and headed back inside. Once they got inside, Wicked was bum rushed by at least one hundred people. All of them that ran up to Wicked were telling him to get ready the shit was about to go down. Wicked looked at his pops and Big Moose said, "Yeah young nigga, you must have forgotten you're going to be out of here tomorrow." Wicked did in fact forget that he was leaving in the morning. Time crept up on everybody and now the time had finally come. All the home boyz in Lancaster, thanks to Big Moose, had put together a going home party for Wicked. I mean for these niggas to be locked up they had more Kush than most niggas on the streets. There was alcohol everywhere. I mean these niggas had it all from Ciroc to Remy Martin. Whatever a nigga wanted you could get it right there at the party. Wicked couldn't believe that his pops had managed to pull this off without him noticing anything. He was impressed with the food these niggas provided. They had gotten some of the COs to show some love and had their broads whip some fly shit together, so you already know his homies were eating well. Young Kats were rapping for Wicked reminding him not to forget about them. Even Big Moose hit some bars and had everybody laughing. The atmosphere was lively, and the energy was even better. Wicked formed strong bonds with some good dudes and felt a sense of loss knowing that he had to part ways with them. One thing was for sure, Wicked wasn't going to ever forget about the partners he has been rocking with in the joint. All his homies were going to be good, and they knew it as well. The party continued all muthafucking night and Wicked knew he has a big day ahead of him. He shook everybody's hand and hugged his pop and told them boyz he would holla in the morning. He walked away from his homeboy and his pops knowing that his destiny was waiting for him and as Wicked prepared to go to sleep, he prayed for the first time in a long time. As Wicked prayed, he asked God to protect him from his friends because he could handle his enemies. Young Wicked fell asleep with the world awaiting his arrival, Demetrious Jones was going home!

Chapter 17:

Free at Last

As the birds started chirping, young Wicked rolled over and opened his eyes and to his surprise, Big Moose has already woken up smiling at his son. Wicked stretched and said, "Damn pop, how long have you been up?" Big Moose looked at his son and said, "Nigga I haven't been to sleep." Big Moose was feeling the effects of his son leaving and now the reality has finally kicked in that Wicked will be walking out that front gate in a couple of hours. Big Moose wanted to make sure he got his last one on one with his son before he left. Wicked said to his pops "You act like you are not going to ever see me again." But what Wicked failed to realize was, after being locked up for over 20 years, seeing your son leave you behind hurts. Even though Big Moose was coming home himself in six months, he was still hurting inside seeing his son leave. Wicked knew it was bittersweet for his pops and he understood how he was feeling, however both men knew that it was show time. Wicked waited for the cell door to open at 6:00 am sharp so he could take a shower and get ready. He came strolling out of his cell door and the whole cell block was up waiting on him. All Wicked could do was smile. He knew that he has touched the lives of a few people. He has gotten close to everybody who was showing Wicked love and all he could do was shake his head.

Wicked stood in the shower and it was hard for him to process that he was going home to his life and family today. He knew that he was a grown man now and would show the world what a grown man looks like. Big Moose watched his son as he got dressed in his prison blues for the last time. Big Moose was proud of his son and the fact that he did ten years and stayed true to form. Wicked hasn't seen anybody outside beside the production team in over ninety days. Wicked told his family and friends that he needed to spend his last ninety days focusing on his mindset. He got dressed and pulled his dreads back into a ponytail. His dreads have gotten so long that they hung on his upper back. Wicked knew that he looked up to par not to mention that he weighed 190 now and he was proud of the muscle mass he had put on. He knew he owed that to his pops who drove his ass crazy on the workouts. He was glad that his pops was there with him. Wicked looked at his pops as he grabbed all his paperwork and said, "Pops, I love you and I'll see you in six months." The two men hugged for what seemed like an eternity then Big Moose wiped a tear away and walked his son to the main building known as "Receiving and Discharge." That's when the white shirts and COs told Big Moose that he couldn't go any further. Wicked stopped and turned to his pops for the last time and said, "Pops, I owe this for the both of us," and at that very moment, Big Moose watched his son go through those double doors to the other side of freedom. Wicked officially left the building and as Big Moose walked back to the housing units, he noticed that the sun had come out of nowhere. He knew that was a sign from God.

It was like a circus where people were outside of the building waiting for Wicked to finally exit. The production team has gained all access to cover Wicked's every move. As the production team made their way to the front of the building, Wicked's mother along with his daughter and Meagan were gathered in front as well. The production team started filming as soon as Wicked took the bag from Meagan and quickly entered the restroom. Shortly thereafter, Wicked came from the restroom and tossed his prison clothes in the trash can. He was wearing a pair of twelve-hundred-dollar Amiri Jeans with the Amiri shirt to match. He also had on a pair of eight-hundred-dollar Black Gucci shoes with a three-hundred-dollar Black Gucci belt. Wicked topped this look off with a pair of gold Cartier glasses. Young Demetrious Jones was ready to make his debut in the world. The production team was on top of every move, and they had Wicked and his family looking like celebrities. Wicked and his family got inside the Back of Black Benz and there were at least thirty cars that were ready to follow. Just before everybody pulled off, Evil and Black met Wicked in the parking lot, and all three men hugged and apparently, they were glad to see each other. There were so many cars, trucks, and vans in the parking lot that the Highway Patrol had to help escort the entourage out into the traffic. So, it was official, Wicked was on his way home. He had the production team follow him and his family to their favorite breakfast spot to eat. As Wicked and his family stopped and ate, the production team filmed every moment of their activity. Everybody was full of life and the people inside the restaurant didn't know what was going on. The owner of the restaurant came to the production team and asked for an explanation. The film director explained to the owner of the restaurant what was going on and who Wicked was. The restaurant owner was handed two thousand dollars from Evil, and everything was good. After everyone was full of all the Japanese food, they left and decided to go to Evil's house in Upper Arlington. Evil has a seventy-five hundred square foot home, and it has plenty of rooms to hold everybody inside and out. Plus, Wicked and Evil agreed that Wicked didn't want anybody to know where he would be living. Once they got to Evil's house, the production team pulled Wicked's mother aside and started to do her segment about being a strong black woman. Wicked couldn't help but admire his mother as she radiated like a queen in front of the cameras. Tina was a natural and she made her kids proud of her and she felt proud to be Wicked's mother. The production team had Meagan and Mariah join Tina and they did a nice family piece as they walked through Evil's home. Everybody was enjoying the moment and Black was happy his partner has finally made it home.

The production team was filming everything and everybody, all Wicked's family members each stood and gave a brief statement about how Wicked was important to them. That was nice and the production team captured everybody as they stood in front of the camera. The production team finally got Wicked, Evil, and Black together and did a piece on the three of them. That piece was called "Forever Loyal." It was a special piece, and everybody felt what Black, Evil, and Wicked had to say but everybody was waiting on the party that was being held at WICKED'S, the club Evil had opened in honor of his homie. Some of the most prominent musicians in the industry were set to attend the party tonight. This party is what the production team had been relying on, and only VIPs were allowed to attend this exclusive party. Wicked sat and joked with people he hasn't seen in years. Willis and the rest of Wicked's siblings all pulled Wicked to the side and they had their one-on-one time. Robyn and Selina both had their one-on-one time with Wicked even though little Mariah wanted her one-on-one time with her daddy too. Tina and Wicked did a one-on-one with the production team. Wicked felt as though everything was going well and he couldn't be happier. Meagan pulled Wicked to the side and whispered in his ear, "When this shit is over, I'm tearing that dick up." Wicked looked at his woman and smiled because he knew she was serious. Wicked had noticed that Meagan was looking exceptionally good. Wicked was thinking the same thing about Meagan as far as what he wanted to do to her at the end of the night. After a few hours, most of the friends and family members that had come to the prison and had been with Wicked most of the day were starting to leave. Wicked thanked everybody for coming and showing their support. He told the ones who were invited to the party that he would see them tonight. The production team told Wicked that they were going to take a break, and the film director told Wicked, Black, and Evil that they would meet with them later at the club. The film director told them that he and his crew would be there an hour before everybody else. So Wicked, Evil, and Black went into a room and discussed their plans for the rest of the day. Black told Wicked and Evil that he needed to run to Cincinnati to handle some last-minute affairs, but he assured them that he and Kesha would be there on time. Evil looked at Wicked and told him to holla at his mother, Meagan, and Mariah because he wanted to take Wicked shopping. Wicked told them that he and Evil were going shopping and he would see them later. Evil was so happy that his partner was back. He went on and on about how much he missed Wicked and how glad he was that Wicked was back home. Evil went into his pocket and gave Wicked a wad of cash and told Wicked that it was for him to have some pocket money. Evil took Wicked to get his ears pierced then he got fitted for suits and Italian shoes. Wicked has a hair appointment at four and he knew not to be late.

It was a sight to see; the production team made every effort to impress. The party had everything that you would see at a red-carpet event and all the major news networks were there. As guests arrived, they were greeted by the valet who parked their vehicles, and then proceeded to walk the red carpet that had been elegantly rolled out for them. Lights and cameras were flashing everywhere. The first car that pulled up was a two-door, all-white Bentley GT Convertible and Black and Kesha hopped out. Black had on a black Burberry London suit, a pair of all-black Giuseppe's with some Prada glasses, and a Prada hat. Black looked like a million dollars. Kesha on the other hand had on an off-white two-piece Louis Vuitton pants suit with a pair of six-inch Jimmy Choo stilettos. She had on some Gucci glasses with a Gucci alligator bag. Kesha looked like Gabriel Union in Bad Boys. As the two of them walked the red carpet, they were stopped by every media station in the State of Ohio. The next car that pulled up right behind Black was Evil and Monique, they were in a black-on-black Aston Martin. Evil was looking sharp as he walked the red carpet in his Cream-colored Tom Ford suit with the cream and black gators on. Evil had on some Fendi glasses with a Fendi hat to match. Monique was wearing a brown striped Louis Vuitton dress. The dress allowed her entire back to be exposed and

Monique's frame complemented the dress. She also wore a pearled necklace that made her look like a movie star. Monique had on some Louis Vuitton shoes and a Louis Vuitton leather purse. Shortly after Monique and Evil were escorted inside, Wicked and Meagan pulled up in a two-door silver Lamborghini. Meagan had on a mint green Christian Dior evening dress that made her look elegant. The dress was strapless, and the back was cut out. Everybody was comparing her dress to the one J-Lo had on when she was with Puff Daddy. Meagan had on a diamond necklace that has over seventy-five diamonds in it. She had on a pair of thigh-high Tom Ford crocodile boots with the crocodile purse to match. Meagan was the best-dressed woman there but not to be outdone by any of the gentlemen in attendance. Wicked pulled off the best-dressed male award. He wore an all-black velour custom-fitted Giorgio Armani Tux. The tuxedo has a dark red trim that ran down the seam of the jacket and pants. Wicked had on a pair of black two-thousand-dollar special made Italian Giuseppe's. He wore a pair of chocolate diamond earrings in each ear. His all-black presidential Rolex watch enhanced his swag.

Wicked had on an all-black, silver Robins hat with silver and gold Robins glasses. Everybody stopped Wicked along his way inside the club trying to get pictures of him and with him was TT and her girls. They were looking good as they escorted every guest inside the club. TT was the talk of the night herself. She wore an eggshell white see-through Valentino Dress, and everybody was saying TT didn't have any panties on and she probably didn't. Nevertheless, TT looked super sexy.

Once everybody was inside, the party officially kicked off and the DJ immediately introduced Waka Flaka and the crowd went crazy. Flaka performed two songs and congratulated Wicked on being home. Before leaving the stage, he introduced Black to the stage. Black got on stage and gave a speech dedicated to Wicked and revealed a special surprise for Wicked. The lights went out and there was a moment of silence, then out of nowhere Rihanna came on the stage and did a dedicated song to Wicked. Rihanna knew that Wicked was one of her most devoted fans and she didn't let the crowd down. Wicked couldn't believe he has this much love and support from people who believed in him. At that moment Wicked understood that he has the world in the palm of his hands. The party was a total success. The film director from the production team had gathered Wicked, Black, and Evil together. The film director went on to explain to them that their crew was leaving so they could start preparing the film. Wicked spoke to Black and Evil and was trying to explain to them that he wanted to leave in a few minutes. He told them that he wanted to leave with Meagan because he wanted some pussy badly! Both Evil and Black laughed at Wicked but understood his frustration now. The DJ had the crowd calling Wicked to the stage and the whole club was screaming Wicked, Wicked, Wicked and Wicked knew he had to get up on that stage because so many people had shown him love. Wicked got on stage and looked at Black as TT and her girls came on the stage. Wicked grabbed the mic and started performing his hit single "Free at Last," the crowd was feeling Wicked as he rocked that stage like he owned it. TT was all over Wicked like she was a part of his outfit, and the rest of the dancers had their shit together. It was an impressive performance and TT whispered in Wicked's ear "That was magic we made on stage wait till I get you in bed, we gone make real magic." Then she licked Wicked in his ear and walked off stage. Wicked knew at that moment that TT had lit a fire inside of him that only she could put out. For the rest of the night, there were several different performances from Trey Songs, Usher, French Montana, and Meek Millz. Wicked made his way to the DJ's booth and announced to the crowd that he appreciated everybody for coming out and showing their support. He told everyone that he had to leave due to other engagements, but he would see them soon at the "Free at Last" album release party. Evil and Black laughed to themselves because they knew Wicked was trying to get Meagan home so he could get some much-needed pussy. After shaking what seemed like a thousand hands, Wicked and Meagan finally made their way out of the club. Now Wicked thought to himself, the only thing that stood in his way of fucking Meagan's brains out was the drive home. The only thing you could hear inside the Lamborghini was the engine roaring.

Wicked had to be doing about 180 because Meagan finally broke the silence and smiled at Wicked and said, "Slow down babe, this pussy isn't going anywhere." Wicked must have been in a zone because he didn't even realize he was going that fast. Nonetheless, they pulled into the driveway of their fifty-five hundred square foot home outside of Washington Courthouse and both Meagan and Wicked started to undress before either one of them got inside the house. Wicked stood in front of his woman and watched her kneel and grab his dick. Meagan was in her panties and bra as she looked up at Wicked sucking his dick. Meagan spit on Wicked's dick and licked it until it was fully stretched out. Wicked stood there with his hands on his head and looked down at Meagan as she pressed his dick up against his stomach and sucked his balls one at a time. Meagan had Wicked going insane but she knew he couldn't take too much more, so she used both hands and took Wicked's entire dick slowly down her throat. Wicked was out of his mind at that point. He took the rest of his clothes off and made Meagan jump in his arms. While Meagan was holding Wicked around the neck she reached back and unhooked her bra. Wicked had already removed her panties and his dick was so hard. Meagan reached behind her and guided his dick inside her wet pussy. Meagan's pussy was so wet that Wicked's dick slid straight to the bottom. Wicked pounded Meagan as she wrapped her legs around Wicked's waist, Meagan screamed out to Wicked as he stretched her pussy with each powerful thrust. Finally, Wicked laid Meagan down on the couch and held her by her ankles. Meagan's ass was hanging off the couch leaving her pussy completely exposed to Wicked's dick. Meagan was feeling so much pleasure and told Wicked to beat her pussy up. Wicked dropped his dick in Meagan's pussy as she screamed out "Get this pussy Wicked, get it," and Wicked power fucked Meagan like that for the next 20 minutes. Then Wicked had Meagan turn around and put her face into the couch and arch her back. Wicked got behind Meagan and put her thighs together and squatted down in the frog position. He slid his dick inside of Meagan from the back barely spreading her cheeks. Meagan went crazy as she told Wicked that his dick was deep in her pussy. Wicked fucked Meagan so long and hard that she thought her pussy was swollen. Wicked told Meagan to get up on his dick and ride it. Meagan damn near out of breath climbed on Wicked's dick and tightened her pussy every time she got to the head of it. Then she would relax her pussy muscles allowing Wicked's dick to penetrate deep in her pussy as she dropped down on his dick. This method drove Wicked crazy, and he pulled Meagan to him as their stomachs were touching. Wicked wrapped his arms around Meagan and held her tight as she told Wicked, she was about to come on his dick. Meagan's nipples were hard as a pencil eraser. Wicked continued to give Meagan nothing but dick as her body tightened up and she exploded all over Wicked's dick. Meagan begged Wicked to fuck her harder and deeper. Wicked held Meagan tight as he told her he was about to cum. Meagan not wanting Wicked to stop told him to come inside her pussy. Meagan knew Wicked's strokes had gotten faster and faster so she knew that Wicked was about to explode. Just then Wicked began to fuck Meagan super-fast and the next thing you know, his body was jerking as he came inside Meagan. Wicked held Meagan in his arms as they fell asleep just like that.

They were awakened by the doorbell constantly ringing. Wicked looked at Meagan and said damn girl you were knocked the fuck out. Evil was at the door and told Wicked he was there to take him to see his PO.

Wicked had lost track of time after that fucking, he put on Meagan's ass. Wicked took a quick shower and told Meagan he would meet her at his mom's later in Cleveland. Wicked's PO was cool and told Wicked he had to report once a month. Wicked left his PO's office feeling good and knew that his probation would be a breeze. Over the next few hours Evil took Wicked sight-seeing and filled Wicked in on all the things that had been going on since he had been gone. Wicked told Evil that he was extremely proud of him, and was glad to call him a brother. Black called Evil had Wicked in the Apple store and got him his brand new, iPhone. Wicked told Black that they would be getting together right after Valentine's Day. Today was February 11th and Wicked had a fresh twenty-four hours of freedom under his belt. Wicked explained to Evil everything that he had planned and what the next move was going to be. Evil understood now that Wicked was home and things were going to be different for him. Evil knew that now everybody was going to be catering to Wicked and doing whatever he said. Evil kind of felt a little jealousy rising inside of him but quickly shook it off. Evil and Wicked drove to Cleveland and spent the rest of the day with Tina and Wicked's siblings. It was around eleven that night and Evil told Wicked that he had to make a run and he would see Wicked after he got back from Houston. Evil had to go check on one of his restaurants in Houston that was having problems with the manager stealing money. Monique was already in Houston waiting for him to arrive. Wicked spent the next two days enjoying his family. Especially little Mariah who loved her daddy more than life itself. Nobody could separate Wicked and Mariah; the two of them spent the next two days hanging out with each other. Every time Wicked would leave with his brother, Mariah would have a fit. Everybody knew that Wicked loved that little girl more than anything on the planet. Meagan kept waiting for the right time to confront Wicked about them finally getting married. Meagan had decided that she was going to present it on Valentine's Day which was the next day. Wicked already promised Meagan that they would spend Valentine's Day together just the two of them. Tina was happy her son was home, and she spoiled Wicked as if he was a baby again. The phone vibrated back-to-back and finally; Meagan answered the phone. Only if Meagan knew that this phone call would change their lives forever. Meagan woke Wicked up and handed him the phone. While Wicked was still half asleep, he looked at the clock and saw it was four in the morning. As Wicked spoke into the phone all he could hear was a whisper. Wicked was confused and said hello who is this? Finally Wicked was able to make out the voice on the other end. Wicked knew it was Evil and asked Evil what was wrong and why he was whispering. Evil spoke with a deep voice and said to his boy, "Damn Bruh, they shot Miracle, and she is fighting for her life." Then he went on to say, "Them bitch ass muthafuckas shot me up." Wicked's mind was spinning like a top and suddenly the room began to spin. Meagan knowing something was wrong, asked Wicked what was going on. Wicked was so shocked by what he was hearing he didn't even realize Meagan was speaking to him. Finally, Wicked spoke into the phone and said where are you? The next thing after that Wicked hung the phone up and told Meagan he had to go to the hospital. Meagan jumped up and said babe I'm going with you. Wicked told her to stay home with Mariah and that he would be back shortly. Wicked arrived at Grant Medical Center and asked the nurse at the front desk where Evil and Miracle were. The nurse referred Wicked to the doctor in charge. After Wicked introduced himself to the doctor, the doctor informed Wicked that they had been expecting him. Wicked followed the doctor to the ICU unit and he saw Miracle with all the tubes running through her little body. The sight of seeing little Miracle in that condition really touched Wicked. At that very moment all Wicked could do was think about killing whoever did this to her. Wicked made his way to the room where Evil was, and Monique was sitting by Evil's side. Wicked stopped and looked at his best friend fighting for his life then looked at Monique and said, "How in the fuck did this happen?" Evil looked at Wicked and said, "Listen Bruh, I know who did this shit to me and my daughter." Evil went on to say I need you on this for real because I can't trust anybody else to handle this shit for me and Miracle. Wicked was furious and all he could do was look at his boy lying there helpless and how he wanted to kill whoever did this. Evil knew Wicked would handle everything so he told Wicked that it should be done fast because the person who did this would be trying to leave town. Wicked leaned down and kissed Evil on the cheeks and told him to consider it done. Wicked told Evil that Miracle was like his daughter, and he swore to Evil and Monique that he would deal with whoever did this shit. Wicked drove back home thinking to himself "How could this happen, and he has only been home four days." Meagan went crazy as she thought about little Miracle and the possibility that she might not make it. Meagan cried for the next hour. Wicked hugged Meagan and said, "Damn babe why does this have to happen on Valentine's Day?"

The End

Here is a sneak preview into the epilogue as you will learn how Evil wants Wicked to back out of his way. The secret about Monique and Wicked being stepbrothers and sisters but the true story unfolds when Wicked learns that Evil is trying to have him killed. Stay tuned for the sequel to LOYALTY IS ROYALTY coming soon, the sequel FOREVER LOYAL....

EPILOGUE

Wicked and Meagan sat at the Japanese restaurant crying and trying to put the tragic events from earlier behind them. Meagan was still visibly shaken thinking about little Miracle and Evil. They had just learned that both Evil and Miracle's surgeries were successful, and both were expected to fully recover. While Meagan and Wicked talked, Meagan reminded Wicked that today was still in fact Valentine's Day. Wicked was supposed to give Meagan an answer about their marriage. Just as Meagan was about to say something to Wicked, his phone started vibrating like crazy. Wicked told Meagan it was Monique blowing his phone up. Meagan told Wicked to answer it. Wicked's face hardened as he listened to Monique's explanation that she needed to see him urgently. He quickly informed Meagan that they had to leave and meet Monique at her house. Monique let Wicked and Meagan in and told them they had better sit down. Monique went straight to the point she looked at Wicked and said, "That nigga lost his mind. Right before he went into surgery, I asked Evil why he called Wicked instead of his so-called goons in Memphis."

Monique went on to say Evil looked at her and said I can't have Wicked coming home taking over everything I worked my ass off to get and now that he's back, everybody will forget who I am and start catering to him. Evil went on saying "Fuck Wicked for real and I'm not about to be under his shadow ever again." Monique was so upset she told Wicked that Evil told her all of this because he had no idea that we were related. Meagan's face turned to stone as she looked at Monique and said, "What the fuck did you just say?" Wicked grasped Meagan's arm tightly and urged her to pay attention. He revealed to her that Monique had discovered they were actually siblings during a conversation he had with his father about six years ago. "Big Moose didn't know that Monique was living in Cleveland and that her mother had lost custody of her. Big Moose used to mess with her mom back in the day and had gotten her mom pregnant and the rest is history. Meagan still was upset because she felt betrayed. Wicked explained to Meagan that when he and Monique found out about their situation, Meagan was happily married to Antonio. Wicked told her that they agreed to keep it a secret. Wicked and Monique both told

Meagan that it was a good thing they did keep it a secret for the best.

However, Wicked sat down and looked at both and said, "DON'T NOTHING BEAT THE CROSS BUT THE DOUBLE CROSS." War is coming!!!!

ABOUT AUTHOR

Maurice Jackson is an aspiring advocate for the youth and the Men and Women of any struggle. Growing up in poverty in Cleveland, Ohio, Maurice had to learn how to survive and care for his younger siblings, a valuable lesson Maurice obtained from his mother (a single mother) trying to raise six kids. Maurice never appreciated being poor or uneducated. So, like most young boys growing up in the ghettos of America, he quickly allowed the neighborhood heroes to raise him. The streets became his second home; the locals became his extended family. Maurice refused to let his shortcomings destroy his dreams of becoming a leader and advocating for better conditions in his community. So, Maurice took to the streets and became a neighborhood hero (himself) by providing for families just like his. However, the law was not on his side. He became incarcerated for being a victim of the "Criminal Justice System."

Nevertheless, Maurice's incarceration allowed him to educate and elevate himself. After serving 24 years and counting, Maurice has transformed his life and has obtained his bachelor's degree in Fine Arts & Communication. Maurice also has an associate's degree in General Studies with a minor in Sociology. But it's not enough. Maurice continues to be a (trailblazer) by establishing self-help programs to assist prisoners with tools to become Men of substance. Maurice Jackson is a prime example of "a setback is nothing more than your path for a greater comeback."

Maurice will be releasing more books under Premeer, LLC. Books to be available include: The Real 80's Baby, The Rise of an 80's Baby, Her Sweetness is Their Weakness, Is it Better to Be Feared or Loved, Sequel to Loyalty is Royalty- Forever Loyal, Queen of the '80s, Big Corey, and lil Corey. Coming soon, be on the lookout for these books.

Contact Maurice @ MooseyDJackson0512@gmail.com

Interested in Writing and/or Publishing a Book?

Visit a2zbookspublishing.net